MW01135590

Project Liberatio

by

Allison Maruska

allisonmaruska.com

Edited by Naomi Hughes and Dan Alatorre

Cover Art: Carolina Fiandri - Circecorp
(www.circecorpwebdesign.com)

A portion of Project Liberatio's sales support Erika's Lighthouse, an organization specializing in recognizing and treating teenage depression.

Advance Praise for Project Liberatio

I love Project Liberatio. Allison Maruska's fast-paced story has truly interesting, 3-dimensional characters and a unique plot that keeps you glued to the page. Sixteen-year-old Rana is especially appealing, and the challenges her older brother Levin endures as a reluctant warrior reach new depth of emotion—and action. The stakes change for everyone as the ultimate battle looms before our genetically enhanced heroes, and how they rise to the challenge is a brilliant and creative ride!

> – Dan Alatorre, author of *The Navigators*

Project Liberatio continues the Project Renovatio story, introducing the reader to new characters and raising the stakes even higher. What I find remarkable about Maruska's imagination and writing skill is both Levin and Rana emerge as compassionate, natural born leaders. Project Liberatio is about our choices and how these choices impact our lives and the lives of those around us. It is a fictional treasure that will fully involve the reader. In addition to being a highly entertaining work, it is thought-provoking. This book will appeal to all readers.

> – Tracy Miller, contributing writer at *The Nerdy Girl Express*

I flew through this book and thoroughly enjoyed it from cover to cover. Allison has a seamless way of writing that really draws her readers in and allows us to experience the story without being bogged down by heavy language. She has turned me into a big fan of hers and I can't wait to read the conclusion to this series!

> – J. H. Winter, author and blogger for *Ink & Stitches*

Game changer Allison Maruska is at it again with this second installment of the Project Renovatio series, and she doesn't disappoint. Maruska takes Liberatio to another level as stakes are raised, heavens fall, and heroes emerge at great costs–the stuff that transforms story to legend.

> – John Winston, author of *IA: B.O.S.S.*

Born and genetically modified to survive the end of days, the Project Renovatio teens found their way into our hearts in the first novel—and are back for more. The author's continuing saga is tightly shaped and moves quickly, with compelling characters and a gripping plot. A gratifying read!

> – Carol Bellhouse, author of *A Ferry to Catch*

<u>Dedication</u>

This book is dedicated to those who read the early drafts and became the trilogy's first fans: Rebecca, Rachael, Emily, Carol, Jael, and Mom, thank you for your excitement and encouragement in those early days. Your support means more than I can say.

Chapter One

Rana shivered as she left the cabin and eased the door shut behind her, careful not to wake the other girls. The chilly Montana morning foretold of an early autumn. Goose bumps formed on her pale skin. She inhaled the dewy air, appreciating the calm that was hard to find among so many of her Project friends. Removing the elastic band from her wrist, she pulled back her black, curly hair and enjoyed the cool breeze on her bare neck.

The sun peeked over the horizon. Someone would see her if she didn't disappear soon, and her alone time would be snatched away yet again. Time to go.

The dirt path crunched under her shoes as she ran towards the forest that sheltered her favorite route. It sounded different than her footfalls on the pavement in her old neighborhood.

Her hand moved to her belly as the increasingly familiar unease took hold.

If she were home now, she'd be training for cross country, studying for her first Advanced Placement history test, or planning this year's laser show with the physics club. She'd likely be tutoring a freshman in math to get some community service hours completed–she would need a lot of those if she wanted a better shot at the elite liberal arts college she had her eye on.

But she wasn't home. She was here, stuck in summer camp indefinitely. Teaching in the little school she'd started for the fifth graders kept her busy, and she could stay in shape for cross country, but everything else was on hold. So much for graduating early.

She ran between the trees and towards the creek, where the trail followed the water's path and periodically crossed over it with log bridges. The first one was within sight. She hadn't been able to run at full speed across one yet, but her balance improved a little each time.

"Rana!"

Keeping her pace, she twisted around and spotted a tall boy with reddish-brown hair. She sighed and slowed a bit, allowing him to catch up.

Jason wasn't a runner, or at least he hadn't been back home. There could only be one reason he'd keep waking early enough to join her. He seemed to have forgotten her sister shared a Project father with him, and dating her sister's brother was too weird to get her head around.

"Did you leave earlier today?" He already sounded winded.

"I don't think so. The sun is just rising later."

She picked up her pace and led the way to the bridge. Why wouldn't he get the hint that she liked to run alone?

Or at least she liked to run alone here. Jacey had finally joined cross country last year, after Rana had badgered her enough. Her best friend ended up posing a formidable challenge in spite of Rana's genetically gifted endurance.

Her stomach knotted again as she reached the bridge. Better not try running across it with Jason behind her; he'd baby-stepped across the thing on previous runs. If he followed her example, he could end up taking an unplanned, icy bath.

His voice broke the silence as she stepped onto the log. "So, what do you think our friends back home are doing?"

She tried not to be annoyed. He missed home, just like she did. He differed from her in that he liked to talk about it.

Holding her arms out for balance, she made her way across the bridge. This would be easier at a faster speed. "Probably just starting to get on the teachers' nerves. I'm sure Jacey is. She's quite the talker."

"Yeah, my friends are probably starting their sports." He grunted as he hoisted himself onto the log. "Or looking for homecoming dates. Or both."

She reached the end and hopped off. "Homecoming? That's not for another couple of months."

"They like to get a head start, or their dates end up being their cousins."

Laughing, she resumed her run. "Homecoming wouldn't even be on my radar." She brushed against a low-hanging branch and wiped away the dew it left behind. "Why are you running, anyway? Your friends are athletes, not you."

"So I can talk to you." He smiled at her.

She offered a polite grin and pulled in front of him.

They ran along a stream for several minutes. Jason fell behind at times, but he picked up his pace and tried to keep up with her.

As the sun rose, setting the moisture hovering around the treetops aglow, they ran in silence. Well– almost in silence. Jason's panting and coughing cut through what would have otherwise been a peaceful run. Maybe she should tell him straight out she didn't want to date him. Again.

As they neared the third and final log bridge, he stopped running and put his hands on his knees. "You're going farther out today. I'm gonna head back. I didn't get the increased endurance gene that you have. See you at breakfast." He smiled, turned around, and walked towards the camp.

She continued across the bridge and down the path, trying to focus on the day ahead, but her thoughts kept returning to Jason.

Why couldn't that guy take a hint? *He* was part of the Project group gifted with words, not her. Although he didn't seem to have a gift in understanding them.

She laughed to herself.

As she neared the dead pine that marked the place she usually turned back, a man sitting on a boulder near the creek caught her eye. Dr. Craig. What was he doing out so early? She slowed and tried to lighten her step, softening the sound of scraping gravel and moving to the grassy edge.

He glanced at her.

Great. Maybe a grin and a nod would be enough for her to continue.

But there was something different about his eyes. Something . . . sad? She crept closer. If he turned away, she'd leave him alone.

He kept his eyes on her. "Good morning, Rana." His jeans, flannel jacket, and beard made him look like a lumberjack, not a top geneticist for a former government research organization.

He returned his attention to the water.

"Hey." She analyzed the landscape as she approached him, trying to discern why he was here. "What's going on?"

"I couldn't sleep."

"Is something wrong?"

"Today's Scott's birthday." He cleared his throat and lowered his head. "Well, was his . . . would have been . . . his birthday."

Oh. This must have been the first birthday Dr. Craig had to experience since both his wife and son had died. She didn't have any words to offer, so she stood next to him and stared at the water.

After several silent minutes, he cleared his throat again. "If I knew a way to get you kids home, but it might be dangerous, what would you say?"

Home? The knot in her stomach untied and transformed into hopeful anticipation, until all of his words registered in her mind. "What do you mean by dangerous?"

"We may have to fight."

"Fight who?"

He stood, nodded towards the camp, and started walking. She followed.

"I can't say much to you now. I'll tell everyone as a group. But there's an opportunity for us to get back, and it may be the only one for some time. In fact, doing nothing could make going home later more difficult."

He sounded like he was thinking out loud, and she tried to imagine the scenario he described. What would make going home more difficult if they didn't deal with it? "If this is our only chance, then we should take it. We should go home."

"I agree. Scott was the reason you're all here." He kept his gaze straight ahead. "It's only fitting that this opportunity would arise on his birthday." Stopping abruptly, he put a hand on Rana's shoulder. "I'll let you go ahead." He trudged back to the rock.

After watching him for a few seconds, she rushed down the path as her head swam.

Home. She could sleep in her own bed, covered by her own blankets, surrounded by her own posters and within reach of her own computer and books. She could invite Jacey over, and they would eat white cheddar popcorn until their stomachs hurt and watch cheesy romantic movies. She could graduate this year, a year early, like she'd planned since seventh grade.

But a lump formed in her throat. Dr. Craig had said "fight." They'd have to fight . . . something. Maybe she should have made him elaborate on his plan before agreeing to go along with it.

****

Levin sat in silence as he finished eating his pancakes and runny scrambled eggs. He looked up when someone patted him on the back and took the seat next to him.

"Hey, bro." Daniel stuffed his mouth with eggs.

Levin scanned the dining hall. Several others had entered. How long had they been there? Dayla and his mother stood in line for food, among the crowd that had arrived without him noticing.

"Oh. Hey."

"Wow, you were really zoning there. What's up?"

Shrugging, Levin focused on his plate. "I kinda thought we'd be home by now. My birthday's coming up. I wanted to spend it with Maggie."

"Oh. Bummer." He took another bite. "We can throw something fun together for you, if you want."

Levin suppressed a wince. Sitting alone in his cabin would be better than a pity party. "Nah, that's all right." He swigged his last bit of juice.

Dayla claimed the neighboring seat, glanced up at Levin, and touched his hair. "Your hair's getting long! It makes you look like Daniel!"

He reached for his wavy hair and touched the small curls at the end. "I haven't felt like cutting it. What do you think? Should I keep it?"

"I like it!" Dayla smiled and took a bite of her pancake.

"Do you want me to cut it for you?" his mother asked from across the table.

"There's no reason to be neatly groomed here. Besides," he turned to his sister, "if Dayla likes it, I think it's worth keeping." He pulled her in for a side hug.

7

She grinned at him with her cheeks stuffed with food.

Liz finished buttering a pancake. "Okay. But don't let it go too much, or you'll end up looking like Rana."

"Yeah, I know. Imagine what Maggie would say."

Dayla laughed.

Levin leaned away from his sister, looking her in the eyes. "What's Rana doing with you guys at her little school?"

She swallowed. "We're reading biographies and doing reports. I chose Martin Luther King Jr. and Janie chose Gandhi. Rana told us to choose someone who fought for human rights."

Levin nodded. "That's a good idea."

Even if Dr. Craig's people were successful in defeating the radical faction of Project Renovatio–a prerequisite for Levin and his siblings to go home– there was always a chance that the true nature of their existence would be exposed. The general population might not like the idea of genetically engineered people walking around among them, and who knows where that could lead? The possibility they would have to fight for their own rights was a real one. Rana was smart to help the younger kids make that connection.

"Have you thought about what you want to do for your birthday?" Liz asked.

"No. I don't think I want to do anything."

She tilted her head. "Really? It's your twenty-first! That's a big deal. We should do something."

"I'm not in the mood to celebrate." He picked up his dishes and delivered them to the kitchen before she could say anything else.

As Levin left the dining hall, Jeremy intercepted him. Levin grinned at his brother in spite of his wish to find a place to be alone and feel sorry for himself.

"Hey. I need to talk to you," Jeremy said.

"Okay. What's up?"

"Not here. Let's go for a walk."

They walked past the cabins and into the forest that guarded the campsite, found a large, flat boulder, and sat on it.

"I was thinking . . ." Jeremy put his hands into his jacket pockets. "What if you and I left? We can go get our girlfriends and find somewhere to hide out."

It was about time Jeremy asked him this. Levin delivered the response he'd practiced, knowing how badly Jeremy must have wanted to get back to his fiancée. "I don't know. What if someone from Scott's group is waiting for us? They know we look like him." He considered Jeremy's tan skin, which Jeremy had inherited from his Cuban mother. "Well, that I look like him, anyway. He had us separated from the rest of the Project kids. I'm afraid we would be the first targets. Just being there would put the girls at risk."

Jeremy's shoulders slumped. "You're right. Of course. We should wait until everyone is safe. I'll see you on the field later, okay?" He stood and walked towards the dining hall.

Levin lay back on the rock, wishing his answer to Jeremy could have been different. He closed his eyes and tried to remember how Maggie looked during those times when she made him blush. He imagined her little half-smile and wide, brown eyes, and he grinned, blanketed by the morning sunshine.

What if he was wrong?

Perhaps no one was keeping an eye out for them. Dr. Craig had said those in Scott's faction were likely recruiting other Project Renovatio families. That wouldn't leave many extra people to monitor the areas where Scott's half-brothers had lived. Then again, no one here had any idea how many people were working for Scott's old faction. They'd been waiting to see if it would fall apart after Scott's death.

That was six weeks ago. If a new group was going to form, wouldn't it have happened by now?

Levin sat up on his elbows, looking towards the parking lot.

****

Rana moved through the craft room that served as a classroom. Her thirteen students–though she didn't like to call them that–read from their biographies and took notes about their subjects.

"How would you guys like to share your projects? Should we take a vote?" She stopped near the front of the room. "We can make posters, dioramas, or we can role-play somehow."

Janie raised her hand, an unrequired school formality that a few kids had trouble giving up. "We should act as the person we're studying! We can talk about them in the first person that way."

"Can we dress like our person? We can make paper hats or clothes if we have fabric," Mallory suggested.

A cheer of approval went up from the children.

Rana held out her hands, quieting them. "That's a fantastic idea. I only have paper right now, so do what you can with that. I'll get some fabric later." She removed a stack of colored paper from a large drawer, and the kids designed hats, bowties, and even facial hair with it, chattering to each other as they worked. She laughed when she imagined having to tape the paper mustaches to their faces.

Rana had created the little school for lack of anything better to do and for a distraction from being stuck here, but as time passed, she found herself looking forward to working with the kids every day. They figured out problems and pieced together their thoughts in ways that would impress her high school instructors.

She could do this for a living–work with gifted kids, or maybe as a guidance counselor for those figuring out their paths.

A wide smile took over her face. Yes. This is what she was supposed to do.

"Why are you smiling?"

She focused on the source of the young voice. Dayla was staring at her, eyebrows scrunched.

"I solved a problem. Don't you feel good when you do that?" Her smiled dissipated. "But it has to wait until we get home."

"When *will* we get to go home?" Dayla asked as she drew an outline of a hat on black construction paper.

She should have been used to these questions, as they occurred more frequently in the past few weeks. The kids had wanted to know why they were here, what they were hiding from, why they were different.

She'd tried to offer the most age-appropriate answers she could.

"I don't know when." She remembered her conversation with Dr. Craig that morning but didn't let that interfere with her answer. "Dr. Craig's people are working to make sure it's safe before we go back."

"But why is it dangerous?" Dayla's question was matter-of-fact. She started cutting out the hat.

Rana stared at the table as she worked out what to say. When she looked up again, about half the class was watching her. She had to say something meaningful. They would know immediately if she veiled the truth.

"You've been working on projects about people who fought for human rights." She walked between the tables, making eye contact with her students. "They fought for people who couldn't fight for themselves, for people who were marginalized, or thought of as less than human." She sat on the edge of the table. By now, all eyes were on her. "You know we're different from normal people, because scientists changed our genes to make us exceptional. Some people out there probably wouldn't like the fact that we exist."

"Why not?" Mallory asked. Her face expressed how ridiculous the idea seemed to her.

Rana stood again. "They'll think we weren't meant to exist, so they could do things to us because they see us as less than human. Or they might think we want to use our gifts to take over society, which is what Scott wanted to do." Hoping to lighten the mood, she brushed the tip of a boy's nose with her finger. "Would you want to be a king?"

He laughed and grabbed his nose.

The small eyes followed her as she moved around the room. "We were created to survive a global catastrophe, not to rule over anyone. Dr. Craig wants to keep us safe from the people who believed like Scott did, because they might use violence to try to control us."

"We have to fight for our rights, like our biography people did," Janie said.

Rana nodded. "Yeah. We might."

****

Levin walked to the side of the mechanical shed. In his life before learning about the Project, he was the resident computer expert. There weren't any computers at the campsite, so he made himself useful by helping his half-brothers with whatever they were doing.

He found Brent's lower half sticking out of the hood of a passenger van. Brent wore shorts in spite of the cooler weather. Levin didn't want to startle him, so he cleared his throat.

Brent pulled himself away from the engine. "Hey, Levin. Th…thanks for coming."

"No problem. What do you need me to do?"

"I'm replacing a b…bent valve," he said. "I'll hand you p…p…parts to keep track of, and you c…c…can hand me the tools I need."

Levin watched Brent work to take apart whatever area of the engine needed the work. He crossed his arms and tried to bury the discomfort in his gut. His brothers could easily transfer their skills to the campsite, giving them obvious ways to pass the time. Brent had his mechanical knowledge, Daniel worked as a camp doctor, and Jeremy formed various exercise groups. Levin had Jeremy teach him Taekwondo just so he'd have something to practice when no one needed his help with anything.

Brent surprised him by starting a conversation from under the hood. "H…h…how have you been?"

"Oh, fine, I guess."

"How's mmmm…Maggie?"

"I haven't talked to her in a couple of weeks, but she said she's doing well. She's busy with school."

Brent handed him an engine part. He put it on a tarp Brent had placed on the ground.

"What about you? How are you handling being stuck here?"

"I w…w…want to go home. I was rrrr…rebuilding a Camaro."

"Really? That's cool!"

"Yeah. I need to p…p…paint it. I'm afraid it will rrrr…rust to death in sss…Seattle." Brent handed him another part.

Levin laughed and put it down. "Do you think there are people keeping an eye on our homes? Like Dr. Craig said? That feels like wasted manpower to me."

"W…wasted manpower?" Brent removed himself from under the hood long enough to shoot Levin a confused look.

"Well, yeah. If they're supposed to be recruiting, having people sit around and wait for us seems like a giant waste of resources. And it's been almost two months. Don't you think they'd give up after a while?"

Brent shrugged and returned his attention to the engine. "I g…guess it depends on how b…b…badly they want to find us."

Levin paced, kicking the dirt. "What if they are waiting? What would they do?"

"They k…kidnapped your mother."

"That was Scott."

Brent emerged from the vehicle again. "If you w…want to go, you should go. No one's mmm…making you stay." He grabbed a small part he'd set on the edge of the frame. "B…but I don't think Dr. Craig w…would keep us here if he didn't have to."

Levin glanced at his car parked in a space behind the van. Sitting there. Waiting for him.

He bit his lip. If he left now, he would get home in the middle of the night. Better to leave early in the morning. Then, tomorrow evening, Maggie would be in his arms.

Chapter Two

Rana sat with her family during dinner, the only meal they regularly ate together. A reminder of home, it had become one of her favorite times.

"So, what did everyone do today?" Liz set a full glass of milk in front of Dayla.

The girl bounced in her seat. "Rana helped us make costumes so we can act like our biography person!" She stopped bouncing and scrunched her nose. "Mine looks funny."

"It doesn't look funny. It looks great." Rana took a bite of her roll.

"My hat looks like a kindergartener made it!"

Levin laughed. "Can't wait to see it." He winked at Dayla.

She stuck her tongue out at him.

Liz distributed napkins to her children, ending with Levin. "What about you? What have you been up to?"

"He took the napkin and crumpled it, keeping it a tight ball in his hand. "I helped Brent fix one of the vans."

"Is that all?" Liz raised her eyebrows.

Levin shrugged and salted his mashed potatoes. "Well, I found a big rock in the forest and took a nap on it."

Rana laughed. "Sounds relaxing."

"It really was." With his fork in hand, he stretched and moaned, making Dayla laugh.

Towards the end of their meals, Dr. Craig, Daniel, Jeremy, and the brother of one of Rana's cabin mates entered the dining hall and made their way to the opposite side of the room. The population of the hall quieted. Dr. Craig stood before the group, while the younger men claimed seats in chairs that had been placed behind him.

Rana held her breath.

"I have news." He clasped his hands in front of him. "Three days ago, one of my people reported that a new leader has taken control of Scott's Project Renovatio faction." He sighed. "That has been confirmed by two others."

The room filled with chatter. Levin placed his elbows on the table and his face in his hands.

Rana shifted in her seat. How was this supposed to get them home? When Dr. Craig had spoken to her about fighting, she hadn't imagined a new leader was involved. How could he think that wouldn't put them in danger?

When the room calmed again, Dr. Craig continued. "His name is Uriah. From what I've heard, he's even more persuasive than Scott was. His group has recruited about thirty Project families to his cause, and their numbers continue to grow. I have reports they're trying to control people in the general population. Of course," he pursed his lips, "this means it will be longer before you can go home."

The chatter resumed as Rana struggled to figure out what he was saying. None of this made sense. He'd said he knew a way for them to get home sooner.

A girl sitting near Dr. Craig shouted over the noise, "What do you plan to do about it?"

"I don't have enough people working for me to effectively face Uriah and his core group of supporters." Dr. Craig's raised voice quieted the group. "And we can't bring in the authorities without the risk of exposing the Project and *you* to the general public. So, we want to organize those of you who are sixteen or older and willing into a force that will face Uriah's group and bring them down."

Levin stood and yelled over the crowd, "You want to turn us into an army to fight the people who want to turn us into an army?"

Rana snapped her attention back to Dr. Craig, bracing herself for his response.

Dr. Craig stepped towards Levin. "Basically, yes. But remember, the goal is completely different. They want to make you into a force to dominate the average population of the country and rise to a level of superiority. We are fighting for your freedom. If– no, when–we defeat them, you can live normal lives, if that's what you want."

Rana's mind hung on "normal lives."

Turning his attention away from Levin, Dr. Craig scanned the group. "If Uriah's people continue to recruit the Project families that are still out there," he pointed towards the door, "they could do some very real damage to our original vision and expose you to the general public. If that happens, you will be outcasts. As those who were never meant to be. Our goal is to keep that from happening." He clasped his hands in front of him again. "The reality is if Uriah's efforts go unchecked, you will not be able to go home without facing danger, either from his group or from the outsiders. Doing nothing is not our best option."

Outbursts sprang up from around the room.

"What are we gonna do?"

"You brought us here and now we'll never leave!"

"How could you let this happen?"

Dr. Craig pulled up a chair and stood on it. "Listen!" He held out his hands, possibly for balance but maybe as a calming gesture.

The crowd quieted, though about half were now standing and glaring at the man who had brought them here.

"Don't forget who you are." Keeping his arms up, he surveyed the room. "You must not forget. Our plan depends on it. Your gifts will get you home."

In unison, a few asked, "How?"

Dr. Craig lowered his hands. "Most of you have experience in a sport. We want you to use your skills to prepare for a combat situation. You'll train for ten days before we decide how to face Uriah's group." He stepped off the chair with a grunt and held his arm out to the three men behind him, who stood. "If you don't have a skill that will transfer well, Jeremy will teach Taekwondo to whoever needs it, and Dante has agreed to help anyone develop their skills in archery. I'd like a few of you to work with Daniel, who will teach you the basics of first aid."

Archery, Taekwondo, or first aid? Rana was clueless about all of those, and she didn't have a skill from home to use. How would she be able to do anything helpful?

Dr. Craig stepped in front of the men again. "In addition, I'll be rotating through the groups to instruct everyone in basic survivalist training, just in case we need to hide out somewhere. If you're not in one of these groups, tell me which group you'd like to join for that training. Are there any other questions?"

A young man in the front stood up. "You expect us to be ready to fight another group in ten days? And won't they have guns?"

Dr. Craig focused on him. "You were created to possess superior strength and intelligence. I have no doubt you can confront another group and win. That said," he returned his attention to the others, "we think you will only need to make an appearance. I want you to have the training in case we face aggression, but I suspect our presence will be enough for us to capture Uriah and turn his supporters. We don't believe they are concentrating their effort in a localized group, per se, so we should outnumber them. As for the guns, the leaders may have them–the officers, if you will–but we doubt any of the recruits will. That would make it too easy for them to fight back and escape if they figure out what's going on."

Rana stood, yelling her question over the crowd. "And what is going on? Why would they join him?"

Dr. Craig nodded to the men standing behind him, and they reclaimed their seats. He took a step towards Rana. "Honestly, we don't know why. Perhaps it would help to imagine yourselves in the place of someone who is learning they're part of PR for the first time. Suddenly, all the skills and talents that set you apart–that made you different–make sense. Then, they say you can use those talents and skills to be important." He held out his hand. "It would be hard for some to turn that down. What they don't see is what you've already learned–they're giving up control. If they figure that out and have the means to escape, they will. Uriah can't let that happen."

Rana put her hand on her hip. "They still have a choice, though. Are these people being brainwashed?" Her question was met with nods and shouts of approval from around the room.

"In a manner of speaking, they are. If Uriah is like Scott was, he's using flattery, manipulation, and straight-out lies to get what he wants. I don't believe your use of 'brainwashed' is an overstatement."

Rana took her seat, but it was uncomfortable. She leaned against her arm on the table.

They could go home, but first they had to fight a group of brainwashed, genetically engineered recruits. And it wasn't supposed to be dangerous.

She scowled and shook her head.

Dr. Craig scanned the room, as if waiting for more questions. When none came, he said, "Make the most of these ten days. This is our best chance to get you home. Jeremy, Dante, and Daniel will be out by the fire pit for the next fifteen minutes."

The crowd started to disperse. Rana waited with her family by the table.

"I don't like this," Liz said from behind her.

Rana turned. Her mother was collecting the dinner dishes. Rana picked up the plates on her side and held them out to her. "This could be our way home, Mom."

Liz snatched the plates from Rana's hand. "You're my children. I'm not going to be excited by the idea of you going to fight a crazy faction leader. It'll be dangerous."

"We have ten days to get ready," Levin said. "Imagine what this group can do with ten days. And he said we probably won't even fight."

Dayla walked over to Levin and wrapped her arms around his waist. He hugged her. When she released, he crouched to meet her eyes. "We're gonna work really hard before we leave. We'll be ready. Okay?" He brushed the tip of her nose with his finger.

She smiled.

Rana stared at her brother, confused by his behavior. This was the happiest he'd been in weeks. In fact, he'd been in a good mood all evening, up until Dr. Craig started speaking. Ironic, considering Dr. Craig was finally offering them a way home.

Liz's words broke her line of thought. "Dr. Craig said those who are willing. You two don't have to go."

"We're a part of this." Levin stood, glaring. "It wouldn't be right to stay here waiting for everyone else to win so we can go home."

Rana took a step towards him. "He's right, Mom. We need to go home. This is no way to live."

"I don't want you to go. Okay?" She shifted her focus from Rana to Levin. "You were hurt last time. You'll be targeted by the guys with guns. I'm sure Dr. Craig will understand if you don't go." She took the dishes towards the kitchen.

Levin rushed to catch up and put his hand on her arm, stopping her. "Mom, I can't stay here anymore." He glanced back to Rana. "None of us should have to. We're supposed to be going to school or building our lives, not hiding out in the woods because someone *might* want to hurt us. Won't things just get worse if we do nothing?"

His mother scowled. "I know you miss Maggie. She'll still be there–"

"Of course I miss her! But it's more than that." He put his hands on his hips. "I want–I deserve–to live where and how I want to live, without having to look over my shoulder for someone who wants to recruit me or for an ignorant person who thinks I shouldn't be alive to hurt me. This has to end. You and Dayla will stay here. Rana and I are going to help us all get home. Even if you make Rana stay, I'm going. I'm an adult. It's my decision."

Liz pursed her lips and turned, disappearing behind the kitchen door.

Chapter Three

Levin twisted the strings of his hoodie as he walked towards the field where Jeremy said to report for the Taekwondo training. The day was cloudy and the chilliest one he'd experienced since they arrived at the camp. It reminded him of waking on autumn mornings, looking out the window, and seeing a layer of the first snow of the season on the ground. When he was a kid, he and Rana would be out playing in it before breakfast.

This time yesterday, he'd planned to be gone by now. That was before the news that he could go home without having to sneak off. Not only that, he could help everyone else get there too. He wasn't about to turn that down.

Jeremy jogged up before Levin reached the group. "These guys are just starting, so we'll be doing things you've already learned. I thought you might like to pick up some basic archery skills with Dante."

Levin flicked his hoodie string. It wouldn't hurt to know a couple of different skills. "That's a good idea. When should I join up with you again?"

"I'll let you know, but I think in a few days, depending on the endurance of this group."

"Okay."

Levin walked up a hill towards the archery range as anxiety took hold in his gut. Before today, he hadn't met several of the other PRs, including Dante. At first, he hadn't thought they'd be at the camp long enough to justify making new friends. After a few weeks, he'd felt guilty for avoiding them, and as more time passed the idea became awkward, as if he'd missed a deadline for introducing himself and doing so now would make everyone uncomfortable. But he had to face them all today.

Several targets attached to hay bales rested at various heights and distances from the shooting line. Dante faced a small group, showing the proper stance for shooting. Levin listened as he approached and hoped he hadn't missed anything important.

Dante pointed to the targets. "Shooting at different distances will develop your accuracy. There's a little wind today, so you'll practice accounting for that as well." He looked up at Levin. "Can I help you?"

Dante's straight, black hair covered the sides of his tan face. Maybe his hair made archery easier for him because it limited his peripheral vision. For half a second, Levin thought Dante and Jeremy might be half-brothers, until he remembered all the halves were connected by the Project fathers, not mothers.

"Is it too late to get in on this group?" Levin asked.

"Not at all. We just started."

Levin stood with the group as Dante continued giving basic instructions on how to load the bow, aim, and fire. Dante gestured to a supply of bows and several quivers of arrows near the center of the shooting line. "I want you to practice with the quiver on your back or at your side, so you'll know how it feels when we need it for real. We don't have time to appropriately measure everyone for a bow, so hold several until you find one that feels natural to you, and try shooting with it. You can trade if needed."

The group members took turns passing around the bows until they each had one they preferred. Before long, they were shooting arrows towards the targets. Levin pulled the taut string–this would take more effort than he'd expected. Following Dante's instructions, he set the nock of the arrow over the string, nearly dropping it, and held up the bow. He pulled back the arrow and aimed for the nearest target. When he released, the string smacked the inside of his arm. The arrow landed in the grass far from the target.

"Ow." Levin rubbed his arm, then reached for another arrow. After a few more shots that resulted in arrows stuck in the ground, he was able to hit his target more often than not. The shooters moved down the line to practice hitting targets at different distances.

As he armed his next shot, Levin tried to bury the reason they were doing this–he might have to shoot someone. Could he do that, if the need arose? His mother had experience with making such a choice: she'd killed Scott to keep him from killing Levin. Did that make the decision to kill easier, knowing she was protecting her own?

He laced his fingers around the nock and fired. The arrow hit the edge of the target, nearly whooshing by it completely.

They weren't practicing in order to protect each other, though. If they wanted to get home, they had to rescue Uriah's recruits from his control and keep anyone else with radical ideas from taking over Scott's mission. It wasn't like when Levin's mom killed to save him. This would be killing for a greater overall purpose, not to directly defend a loved one. Could he do that? Could he look someone in the eye, arm his weapon, and fire with the intention of ending a life?

Sighing, he shook off the thought as he loaded the bow again. For now, this was a hobby. Dr. Craig had said they wouldn't likely have to fight. So this was simply broadening his skill set.

As he positioned himself to take the next shot, a familiar voice said his name and startled him. His arrow planted itself in the ground embarrassingly far from the target.

"Good thing we have ten days." Rana laughed as she approached.

"I would have made it if you hadn't surprised me." Levin plucked another arrow from the quiver at his side and shot again, this time hitting the target with a solid whack.

"That's better."

Dropping the bow to his side, Levin faced her. "Do you need something?"

"It's lunchtime. I'm supposed to come tell you guys."

"Oh, okay. Thank you," Dante answered. Levin hadn't noticed him walk up behind him. Sneaky guy.

Levin put away his supplies and walked with his sister. With her hands in her pockets, she exhaled into the chilled air and watched her breath dissipate. "I thought you were training with Jeremy."

"They were doing things I already learned, so I came up here."

"Are you gonna keep doing this?"

"Wouldn't hurt to train in two skills." He put his hands in his pockets. "What about you? What are you training in?"

"I kept school going this morning." She sniffed. "I don't know if I'll be going with you guys to fight Uriah."

Levin stepped in front of her and glared. "You have to come with us. We need all the people we can get."

"But I'm not trained in anything useful. Except running away." She laughed.

"Do first aid with Daniel. Come on, you have to do something."

She walked past him. "If I go, and if something happens to me, who will take over the school here?"

"If we win, we won't have to come back here and the kids can go to their regular schools. And don't you want to get home? Graduate early, do cross country . . ." He raised his eyebrows.

"Of course I do." She kicked the dirt.

"We have a better chance if everyone's on board."

She pursed her lips. "I'll talk to Daniel after lunch."

****

"Hey, can you give me a ride into town?" Daniel took a bite of his chicken sandwich.

Levin set his plate on the table. "Sure. Why?"

"I need to pick up some more supplies. Four kids said they wanted to do the first aid training. I wasn't planning on that many."

"Oh. Well, you're gonna have a fifth."

"Do you want to do it?" Daniel scrunched his eyebrows.

"No. Rana."

"Really? I thought she wasn't going."

"I talked her into it."

Daniel grinned. "Janie told me Rana said something to them about us fighting for our rights. She wants to come with us."

Levin chuckled. "She must have missed the 'sixteen or older' part."

Dante approached their table and stood across from Levin, holding his own tray. Between two fingers, he held an ancient-looking stone arrowhead. "Mind if I join you?"

Surprised, Levin leaned away. Most guys would just plop down wherever they wanted. "No. Have a seat."

He sat and bowed his head, mouthing inaudible words before picking up his fork. In his other hand, he weaved the arrowhead between his fingers. "So, Levin, you seem to have a natural talent in archery. I don't know if you noticed, but you hit the target at least twice as often as the others. Have you shot before?"

"Really? No, I didn't notice. And no, I'm an archery novice."

"Interesting. I'm glad to have you in the group."

"Thanks, but I might not be staying." Levin explained the situation with Jeremy's group.

"I see." Dante nodded. "But I think you'll be quite accurate in just a few days, possibly even a leader in the group. Keep that in mind."

A leader? Levin stopped chewing. "Okay." When the surprise wore off, he asked, "How long have you been shooting?"

"About eleven years. My dad–my mom's husband–started taking me bow hunting when I was seven. I got bored waiting forever for animals, so I started shooting other things–pinecones, cattails, things like that. Once, I shot a squirrel and yelled in triumph!" He raised his arms and laughed. "I scared the buck my dad was tracking. He was so mad." He chuckled as he took another bite. "Anyway, when he settled down, he saw that shooting the squirrel took real accuracy. He enrolled me in archery classes and I started competing. I'm going to the next Olympic trials."

"Wow. Will you be on TV?"

"Probably not." Dante chuckled again. "I'll have to get through a few rounds before I get to be on TV." He sipped his water. "This is different though. I hope you guys won't find yourselves in a position where you have to use the weapon on a person." He scratched his head with the arrowhead point.

Levin wiggled his fork in his hand. "What about that? Do you think you could do it? If you had to?"

Dante nodded. "If I was protecting someone in danger, yes. Though it wouldn't be easy." He glanced at the ceiling, as if thinking through something. "When bow hunting, you want to aim for a kill shot, so the animal doesn't suffer. If you hit the leg it could hobble away, and you have to track it before predators get it." He sipped his water again and shook his head.

Staring, Levin waited for Dante to elaborate. "You're thinking we'll need to learn kill shots. On people."

He tapped the arrowhead on the table. "It wouldn't be a bad idea to learn them, just in case. Will we need to use them?" He shrugged. "I hope not."

Chapter Four

Levin drove Daniel into town, and when they reached the drugstore, Daniel pulled a wad of cash from his pocket.

Levin's eyes widened. "Where did you get that?"

"I robbed a convenience store. Was that wrong?" He smirked. "What do you think? Dr. Craig gave it to me. You need anything?"

"That's a lot of cash. What are you getting?"

"Stuff for suture kits, mostly. We don't know what we'll be walking into." Daniel counted the bills.

"Dr. Craig said we were just making an appearance." Levin said the words more to convince himself than to argue with Daniel. After his conversation with Dante and now this sudden need for first aid supplies, the situation could realistically call for them to do more than simply show up and look scary.

"There's the possibility of aggression. Better to be prepared." Daniel left the car.

Levin watched him enter the store, wishing he hadn't been so insistent on Rana going with the group.

Remembering the other reason he came into town, he pulled his phone from his pocket. He hadn't talked to Maggie in weeks. Not wanting to keep a line open, he sent her a simple text, though even a texting conversation could be traced, if Uriah's people were paying attention.

Hey beautiful.

He waited a minute before she replied.

Hey! I'm so glad to hear from you! How's it going?

We're going to fight. Hoping to be home soon. He winced. That bit of information might have been too much for anyone spying on them.

He stared at the screen, waiting an uncomfortable length of time for her reply. What was she writing?

Fight?

That was it? *Yeah. Can't go into details. See you soon. I love you.*

He clicked off his phone and genuinely smiled for the first time in longer than he could remember. *See you soon.* It was true. He would see her soon–though he couldn't say how soon or what he might have to do to get there.

****

After twenty minutes in Daniel's group, Rana knew it wouldn't work. Daniel's detailed and graphic explanation on the differences between a venous bleed and an arterial bleed made her nauseated, and she had to focus her attention on the tiled floor of the small medical room. She glanced at one of the two beds set against the adjacent walls. Would anyone judge her if she lay down on it?

Closing her eyes, she tried to refocus. This was her ticket home. If they did end up in a fight, what she learned here could keep her friends in it as long as it took to win, or she could even save someone's life.

She forced her eyes open again as Daniel held up a severed pig leg and explained how a tourniquet stops gushes of blood from squirting out and killing the victim. Her stomach turned, and she wrapped her arms around it.

"Are you okay? You look p...p...pale," Brent whispered to her.

Daniel threw his hand out from his body again and again, pretending it was a stream of blood. "Sometimes the body will quiver and jolt with involuntary convulsions. This is a sign of the victim 'bleeding out,' or fighting 'de manu mortis,' the grip of death—so you must act quickly. Obviously, that makes it harder to tie the tourniquet. The victim's blood will spray you . . . ."

Shaking her head, Rana stared at her lap. "Not really. I don't think I can do this."

"Wait until we're p...p...practicing. It gets better."

She focused on the light reflecting off the floor and took a long breath. "I'll try."

Daniel handed out sticks, shirts, shoelaces, and bandanas to practice tying tourniquets with a partner. He walked around and put stickers on limbs to represent where the pretend arterial bleeds were, placing a sticker just above Rana's knee. Brent positioned a stick and tied a bandana around her thigh above the sticker.

Rana watched him work. "I don't know if I could do this with blood spurting at me."

"I th…th…think you wouldn't notice if someone needed you. You know how to take care of people."

She grinned.

Daniel put a sticker on the inside of Brent's arm between his elbow and shoulder. Rana grabbed a shoelace and tied it beneath his armpit. "I hope you're right. I hope he doesn't want to teach me how to do stitches."

"We mmmm…might have to."

An image of her fingers pulling thread through someone's skin flashed in her mind–actually, they were Daniel's fingers, and he was stitching Levin's wound the night before they came here–the black thread sliding through her brother's flesh as he held his breath.

Her stomach turned again, and she grimaced.

Brent put his hand on her shoulder. "If you w…want to leave, do it. We need p…p…people who won't lose it in r…r…real life."

She swallowed as Daniel circled the room, smiling and offering guidance to her friends.

If she left, what would she do? If they all wanted to go home as badly as she did, they would do anything they could to help. It was too late to jump into another group. Maybe if she practiced more, like Brent said, her queasiness would ease. "No. I'll stay."

****

When Levin and the archery group returned to the range, a pair of siblings with dark brown skin claimed the target on the end and threw rustic spears at it. The girl hit the center of the target nearly every time, and Levin stood in awe as he watched her. She must have competed in the decathlon in her normal life. Dr. Craig had said they could use any sport to face Uriah's group. How many other sports would be represented?

Levin reloaded his bow after the break. He hadn't hit the middle of the target, and after watching the girl do it effortlessly, that became his new goal. As discomfort grew in his gut, he fired again, hitting the bottom of the hay bale.

How would this work in a fight if he couldn't even hit a stationary target in practice?

"Can I help?" Dante stood close behind him.

"I dunno. I just want to hit the center. That girl with the spears makes it look so easy."

Dante laughed. "Don't worry. Amaya's been throwing javelins for a while. You'll get there. Are you hitting the low end of the target?"

"Yeah."

"Then aim higher than you think you need to." Dante walked to another archer.

His cheeks burning, Levin aimed his arrow, tilted upward a bit, and fired. The arrow hit the target dead center.

"Nice shot!" Amaya yelled.

"Thanks." He smiled at his accomplishment.

After a few more shots, Dante called the group together. He held a large, black garbage bag full of . . . something.

"We need to start practicing on another level." He reached into the bag and removed a Styrofoam head, like one a costume shop or wig store might use, and pointed to the neck. "There are places on the body you want to aim for, to . . . keep the person from fighting back. The neck is a good one, but it's a small target. Easy to miss." After setting the bag and head down, he entered the storage shed and returned dragging out a beat-up mannequin. "When game hunting, we aim for the lungs." He swept his hand in a circle in front of his chest. "The bigger target is easier to hit, but if you miss, you're more likely to strike a vital organ or blood vessel in the torso. This would be the best course for us as well."

"Hold on a second." A blonde girl who looked Levin's age raised her hand. "Do you really think we'll have to do this on people? Does Dr. Craig?"

"Realistically?" Dante shrugged. "We don't know what we'll be walking into. If Uriah's men are armed, it may be up to us to take them out before they can hurt one of us." He leaned the mannequin against the shed. "If any of you feel you won't be able to use your skills like this, it would be best to find another way to help. We need everyone we can get, but it would be dishonest of me to say there's no way we'd have to shoot a person. I simply can't predict that. No one can. If you can't handle the possibility, bring me your bow and move on. No hard feelings."

Dante stood before the perfectly still group, all eyeing him. Levin gripped his bow tighter.

****

Three days later, as Levin finished breakfast and mentally replayed some of his better shots at the hay bales–not at the Styrofoam head or the mannequin, though–the sound of singing female voices reached him. His mother and sisters were approaching his table; Dayla carried a glazed donut with a lit candle sticking out of it.

A smile took over his face. It was his birthday. He'd completely forgotten.

The three stopped at his table and finished the worst rendition of "Happy Birthday" he had ever heard. Laughing, he ignored the heat rushing to his face and blew out the candle. "Thanks."

Liz handed him a napkin. "Sorry it's not a cake. It's the best we could do."

"Oh no, this is enough embarrassment, thank you." He put the candle on the table and took a bite from the donut. The soft, sugar-coated treat melted in his mouth, and he eagerly took the next bite. He couldn't remember the last time he ate a donut.

The girls joined the line to get breakfast. Over the course of the next ten minutes, his half-brothers visited his table to wish him a happy birthday. He had to beg Daniel not to sing to him again.

"I wish we could take you out for an appropriate twenty-first birthday celebration." Jeremy winked.

"Thanks. Maybe after we get out of here." It would be nice to do something fun in public with his brothers, but only Dr. Craig's people, Levin, and a few others went into town, and even they didn't go there more than once per week. Dr. Craig didn't want to raise the suspicions of the townspeople.

Jeremy leaned into his arms on the table. "The Taekwondo group is coming along more quickly than I expected. You can rejoin today, if you want."

"Let me think about it. I'm doing pretty well with the archery."

"Okay. I wouldn't come at all if you don't come today, though. Tomorrow, you'll be behind."

Levin toyed with the idea. It would be better to be as fully trained as possible in one skill than to be marginally trained in two, and he had more experience with Taekwondo. "All right. You talked me into it."

Jeremy smiled. "Great. See you there." He hopped up from the table and joined the breakfast line.

Levin stopped by Dante's table on his way out of the dining hall to tell him about rejoining Jeremy's group. Dante told Levin he could shoot in the evenings if he wanted to.

That night, Levin shot dozens of arrows in an effort to keep his mind off the fact that he wasn't with Maggie. Tiny snowflakes floating through the air–the first snow of the season, reminding him of his first date with her. It had been snowing that night.

An uncomfortable mix of anxiety and longing took hold in his gut, and as a lump formed in his throat, he fired the arrows more rapidly. Fewer and fewer of them hit the target.

He had to get back to her, and when he did, he'd make sure they wouldn't have to separate again. All he had to do was ask her.

The ache in his gut immediately eased with his decision.

****

Rana continued to teach at her school in the mornings, and Brent caught her up when she joined Daniel's group in the afternoons. Her unease lessened the more she practiced, as Brent had predicted. They agreed to work as a team through the training and when they faced Uriah.

A week after Dr. Craig's announcement about Uriah, Daniel decided the group should learn how to do sutures. He'd had trouble finding human-like specimens for them to practice suturing, so Dante's team had shot some birds, squirrels, and a rabbit for him.

Each pair received a bird or squirrel that Daniel had balded and cut in various places.

"Everyone will get a kit containing lidocaine gel and suturing supplies. We learned the hard way how important a numbing agent is the night we came here." Daniel winced a little, likely remembering how he had to stitch Levin's chest wound that night. "If you don't numb it, the person will feel every insertion of the needle and pull of the thread. It's very unpleasant. But if you have to stitch someone and don't have anything to numb the area, stitch them anyway. It's better to clean and close the wound to prevent infection than to leave it open."

Daniel had everyone surround a table, and he demonstrated his suturing technique on a squirrel before setting the pairs off to practice. Rana and Brent took turns suturing and assisting. As Rana worked, she recalled Levin's experience: he had to endure ten inches of un-numbed stitching. She shuddered.

"Is sss…something wrong?" Brent leaned towards her.

"I just have a whole new respect for Levin now."

Brent nodded. "Yeah."

She finished on her animal and handed over her supplies for Brent to take his turn. Watching him work the fine thread with his mechanic hands, she tried to keep herself from imagining a scenario that would require them to use these skills.

Chapter Five

"Levin, do you have a minute?" Dr. Craig stood at the edge of the field as the Taekwondo group finished their afternoon practice. He drummed his fingers on his leg, and his eyes darted from one Project kid to the next.

"Sure. What's up?"

"Let's go for a drive. Do you have your keys? It would be easier to take your car than one of the big vans."

Levin scrunched his eyebrows. "Yeah. They're in my cabin. I'll meet you in the lot."

After retrieving his keys, Levin settled into the driver's seat next to a silent Dr. Craig. "Where am I going?"

"Just head into town." Dr. Craig dropped the seat belt as he pulled it across his body, causing it to smack the door. As he fumbled for it again, he successfully inserted it into the latch. Sighing, he clasped his hands in his lap and stared out the windshield.

Levin eyed him suspiciously. "Is something wrong?"

Dr. Craig shook his head and pointed. "Let's go. We're on a schedule."

Easing the car down the long driveway leading away from the camp, Levin waited for the old man to explain. "Wasn't there something you wanted to talk about?"

"Yes, but not yet. Wait 'til we get there."

"Get where?"

"Just keep driving."

Levin hovered his foot over the brake pedal. Dr. Craig hadn't asked any of them to do anything without a full explanation before. What had to wait until they got there–wherever "there" was? Was he setting Levin up for something?

He moved his foot back to the accelerator. Dr. Craig wouldn't start behaving in a way that would harm them. He'd sheltered them, after all. Whatever this was about, he must have had his reasons for doing it this way.

When they reached the town, Dr. Craig pointed. "Pull up next to the park. We're meeting someone there."

"Who?"

"Just . . . you'll see."

Levin parked and faced his passenger. "What's going on? Tell me, or I'm going back to the camp right now."

"There's something I need to do, and I feel like I can trust you knowing about it." He scanned the park. "Only one person can know. If you don't want the responsibility, tell me. We'll go back and I'll get

43

someone else." He checked his watch and scowled. "I'd rather not, though. We don't have much time left before we leave the camp."

"Much time for what? We're not leaving for three days."

Dr. Craig shook his head. "We have to leave tomorrow."

"Tomorrow?" Levin sat up straighter, glaring. "Why didn't you tell us? Ten days of training might not have been enough. Eight could be suicidal."

"I doubt two extra days would make a difference."

"You mean we'll lose either way." Levin put his hands on the wheel and focused ahead. "Fantastic."

The old man cleared his throat. "I don't expect you to lose because I don't expect us to fight."

"What if you're wrong?" Levin squeezed the wheel.

"Wrong?"

"Why are the archers learning kill shots? And why teach us survival skills?" Levin twisted his body to face Dr. Craig. "You *do* expect us to fight. You just don't want to tell us because you think we'll lose and have to hide." Dread covered him–were they walking into a hopeless battle?

"If I thought any of that, we wouldn't be going." He unfastened his seat belt. "In any case, we have to leave tomorrow. We don't have a choice. I found out two hours ago. This meeting was supposed to happen in a couple of days. We're lucky Richard can meet us on short notice."

"Richard?"

"You'll see. Come on."

Before Levin could insist on further explanation, Dr. Craig left the car and walked towards the sidewalk.

Levin yanked his keys from the ignition and rushed to meet him. "Do you think this is something I can handle? Or was I the first person you saw on a tight schedule?"

"You can handle it. There's just one thing you need to know going in: don't mention PR to him."

Levin scowled.

"I'll explain why after the meeting." He turned and hurried into the park, towards a man sitting on a bench. The stranger wore a dirty plaid shirt with the sleeves rolled up and faded denim shorts, and his silvery hair hung in thin strands around his face. As they neared the bench, he stood.

"Steven! How are you?" The man shook Dr. Craig's hand. Levin was surprised to see the man had perfect teeth. His voice was firm with a slight southern drawl.

"Oh, hangin' in there. I want to introduce you to the young man I told you about. Richard, this is Levin Davis." He clasped Levin's shoulder. "Levin, this is Richard Blake. He's a local attorney."

Attorney? "Nice to meet you." Levin shook Richard's hand.

"Likewise. Should we walk?"

The three strolled down the path. Dr. Craig twisted his watch as he spoke. "I'm afraid I had to spring this on Levin about twenty minutes ago, so he doesn't know why we're here. I was hoping you can fill him in more eloquently than I could."

Richard laughed. "Well, I don't know about that, but I'll give it the old college try." He occasionally glanced at the path while he focused on Levin. "Son, are you aware that Steven owns the campsite you're living on?"

"Yes."

"Okay. He placed the property in a trust, along with a significant sum of money that I control. Its purpose is to secure the long term sheltering and maintenance of a large group of people, such as the one you're currently with."

"Why do I need to know this?"

"I heard you're all leaving tomorrow and not planning to return."

Levin frowned. "A lot of us are leaving." He looked past Richard, towards a young couple on the other end of the park. The girl had straight brown hair, like Maggie's. He had to look away.

"Right. Steven set this up as a safety net. In case you need to come back." He pulled an index card from his shirt pocket and held it out to Levin. "I'm authorized to grant you access to the site and release the money to you as you need it. My number is on this card. Keep it somewhere you won't lose it."

Levin took the card and examined it. "But why can't Dr. Craig just control it?"

"This is in case something happens to me and I can't come back here with you," Dr. Craig said.

"In case something happens to you? And I'm the only one who knows about it? What if something happens to me?" Levin couldn't make sense of Dr. Craig's actions–the camp, the money, or his statement–how would anything happen to him when the PRs were the ones training for a fight? And if they had to come back here . . .

Levin grimaced at the thought. He couldn't come back here. He wouldn't.

"Levin, I chose you for a reason. We need to keep it quiet. The more people that know, the more likely the information will get out, and that means the government will get involved. If that happens, they'll know where all the PRs . . . where you all are, and that would put you in danger."

"Yeah, we best keep the government out of our affairs." Richard put his hands in his pockets.

"Richard, please," Dr. Craig said.

Richard raised his eyebrows. "I'm just saying."

Dr. Craig returned his attention to Levin. "I'm doing this because if it becomes necessary, you can all live here in safety. I figure the chance of something happening to both of us is slim."

"So if we end up back here without you, I'm supposed to call this number." Levin folded the card and put it in his pocket.

"Exactly." Richard nodded.

"I really don't think that'll happen." Levin couldn't stomach the idea of pulling out of his life again.

Dr. Craig pursed his lips. "I hope not. But like Richard said, it's a safety net. Use it if you need it." He stepped in front of them and shook Richard's hand. "Thanks for your time. We'll be on our way."

****

"What the hell was that?" Levin asked as soon as he and Dr. Craig re-entered the car.

"Drive."

"Tell me."

"I will. But we need to get away from the town first. I don't want to draw attention."

Levin drove towards the camp for five minutes before Dr. Craig spoke.

"Richard doesn't know about PR. He thinks I'm sheltering a group of abused runaways."

"Do you really think we'll have to come back here?"

"All you need to know is this is a backup plan. Richard lives off the grid, so no one can track you through him. Should the safety of the PR kids be jeopardized again, like it is with Uriah, this is where you can seek refuge."

"Like if the public learns about us?"

"Precisely." He paused. "Or if another group decides they don't want you around. It's the same reason I've been going from group to group teaching survival skills. They're just in case, but you likely won't need them."

Levin cocked his head. "What other group? And what was all that about the government?"

"PR is government funded. I don't want them to find out where you are through another government agency, like the IRS. Richard's very anti-government. It's one of the reasons I hired him. Unless I can take back control of the organization, we can't assume anyone in any departments will sympathize with us."

"But why would the rest come back here if I'm the only one who knows about this?"

"They can know to come back. But they can't know about the trust or about Richard. That's all on you."

Levin stopped the car in the middle of the dirt road leading to the camp. "Why me?"

Dr. Craig faced him. "The night I told everyone about Uriah, you asked why I would use you all to form an army to fight the group who wanted to make you into an army. I knew then that you were the man I should choose to carry this responsibility. You look out for your siblings and your friends before anything else."

"I don't know about that." He started driving again. Did this guy know Levin hadn't learned everyone's names until a week ago? Or his primary reason for going along with the training was to get back to Maggie? "You didn't answer my question. What other group?"

His hand went to his watch. "I can't say right now. You'll just have to trust me. I'll tell you more if I think you need to know."

Levin bit the inside of his cheek. Whatever Dr. Craig was hiding could have something to do with the group's safety. Why wouldn't he tell what he knew now, especially to the person he'd put in charge?

Chapter Six

As Levin and the others finished breakfast, Dr. Craig stood near the door of the dining hall. He'd told them at dinner the night before they would be leaving today, but he hadn't offered much more information than that, saying he was still gathering intelligence. Levin's nerves crowded out most of his appetite, but he forced himself to eat. The snacks he packed wouldn't last long if he got hungry on the road from intentionally missing a meal.

Dr. Craig cleared his throat, and the crowd quieted. "I have more information about our plan. Uriah's supporters are most concentrated around San Diego and Denver. We believe Uriah is in Denver, so we'll head there first and go to San Diego if needed."

Levin's nerves irritated his stomach. He was going home, but dangerous people were close to Maggie. Their proximity would make it more difficult for Levin to get to her.

"It will take about twelve hours to get there, so we'll arrive late tonight. I've arranged for a hotel to allow us to sleep on cots and bedrolls in one of their ballrooms. I told them we're a high school drama club traveling for a competition. Tomorrow, we'll get a better idea of where Uriah's people are and how to . . ." He paused as if looking for the right word. "Engage them. Anyone who's coming, meet at the van in two hours. Don't forget to bring your weapons and personal belongings." He walked out the door.

Daniel looked at Levin. "Denver! Can you believe that?"

"Why are they there? I don't like how close to home they are." Levin crumpled his napkin.

"Who cares? If we beat them in Denver, you can just stay there!"

Levin hadn't considered that. If everything went well, he could safely be with Maggie tomorrow night.

With the burst of adrenaline, he left the table and rushed to his cabin to gather his belongings.

****

Rana hoisted her duffel bag onto her shoulder and shut the door to her cabin, scanning the grounds one last time before heading to the van. As she stepped towards the parking lot, Dayla's voice stopped her. "Rana!"

The girl ran across the field, followed by her leisurely strolling mother. Dayla was smiling, but when she hugged Rana, she squeezed much harder than normal.

Rana grunted. "Okay. I think I'm hugged out."

Dayla squeezed tighter, so Rana tickled the girl's ribs.

Her sister laughed and wiggled away. "Stop!"

Rana delivered one last tickle. Dayla shrieked before a scowl took over her face. She crossed her arms.

Putting her finger under Dayla's chin, Rana looked into her sister's eyes. "We'll be okay, girlie. You know that, right? Dr. Craig wouldn't lead us into something dangerous."

Dayla nodded.

"You want to go home, right?" For Rana, the anticipation of going home had become more pronounced in the past few days, and after Dr. Craig told them they were leaving today, she did an extra run around the camp to burn off the excitement.

"Yeah." Dayla put her hands in the pockets of her jeans. "I don't want you to get hurt. Like Scott cut Levin."

Rana stroked Dayla's hair. "Don't worry. We're all gonna take care of each other. I'll help anyone who gets hurt, like Daniel helps people."

Dayla smiled.

"I need to say goodbye to Mom now. Why don't you go find Levin and say goodbye to him? I think he's by his car."

"Okay." She hugged Rana, more gently this time, and headed towards the parking lot.

Liz took Dayla's place and embraced her daughter. "Please, be careful."

After releasing the hug, Rana kept her hands on her mother's shoulders. "I will. Did you hear what I told Dayla, or do I need to repeat it?"

Liz laughed as a tear escaped. "I'm so proud of the young woman you're becoming."

"Thank you. We'll be fine. And we'll be home soon." Rana hugged her again.

"Can you do something for me?"

Rana nodded.

"Keep an eye on Levin."

Rana scrunched her eyebrows. "What do you mean?"

Liz glanced at the parking lot. "He's so determined to get to Maggie. I'm afraid he'll do something to endanger himself and the group."

"I'm not sure I'd be able to stop him if–"

"Just try, okay?"

Rana blinked a few times. "Okay." Levin hadn't needed her protection before, especially from himself. Her nerves gathered in her stomach. "Why are you worried? Did he say something?"

Her mother shook her head. "I just have a feeling. He's so in love with her. He'll do anything to get to her." She grinned and put her hands on Rana's cheeks. "I love you." She kissed Rana on the forehead and followed Dayla towards the parking lot.

Rana said, "I love you, too," unsure if her mother heard it.

****

"Levin?"

His little sister's voice pulled him from the trunk of his car, where he was organizing his and his brothers' belongings. "Oh, hey, Dayla."

She reached into her pocket and pulled out a paper she had folded to a small rectangle. "I made you this. For good luck." She held it out to him.

"Oh. Thanks." He took the paper and unfolded it. "Can you tell me about it?"

She pointed to the pictures as she spoke. "This is a bow and arrow, because you were practicing with those. This is my Martin Luther King costume, because you thought it was funny, and this is you and Rana."

He laughed when he saw "long hair" with an arrow pointing to the picture of his head. He read the message aloud. "'Be careful. I'll miss you.' Aw, that's sweet." He hugged her. "Thank you. I'll keep it with me all the time." He meant it. It's wasn't every day he received a personally delivered good luck charm.

She smiled. "Okay. But don't show Rana. I didn't make her one."

"Why not?" He cocked his head.

"Because you got hurt last time. I thought you needed good luck."

He laughed at her practical explanation as Liz approached.

Leaning in, he whispered, "Should I hide this from Mom, too? She's heading this way."

Dayla's eyes widened and she nodded. Levin smiled, folded Dayla's note, and put it in his pocket.

****

Grateful he was allowed to drive his own car, Levin followed the third van at a respectable distance. While he wanted to speed to Denver and to Maggie as quickly as possible, passing everyone would do nothing but raise questions he didn't want to answer. With his half-brothers riding with him and providing ample conversation, the trip would pass quickly, even through the flat, boring parts of Wyoming. They would reach Denver in less than a day.

His leg mindlessly bounced with anticipation.

"How did everyone's training go?" Jeremy stretched his arms in the passenger seat as the camp disappeared in Levin's rear-view mirror.

"Really well." Daniel looked up from his book. "I covered a lot more than I planned. What do you think about it, Brent?"

"It was r...r...really good. But I hope I don't have to use what you t...t...taught me."

Levin chuckled. "Yeah, me too."

Jeremy whacked Levin's shoulder. "And I guess Levin is the multi-tasker here."

"I just hope I can figure out how to use what at the right time."

"I wouldn't worry about that. You made great progress in the Taekwondo exercises. And from what Dante said, you practiced shooting every night. Did you bring a bow and arrows?"

"No, but I think he packed all the ones we had. I'd rather not carry extra stuff around."

The men traveled quietly for a few minutes, until Daniel broke the silence. "What will we do if they have guns?"

No one answered right away. Levin was sure they had all thought about it, but since they weren't able to train with firearms without bringing unwanted attention to the camp, they didn't dwell on that possibility.

"I guess we hope we outnumber them enough for them to surrender, or we can shoot them with arrows first or kick the guns out of their hands." Levin winced at the lame explanation. The truth was they might not know who had guns until it was too late–

Dr. Craig had said only the leaders in Uriah's group would have them, but Levin and his peers couldn't know for sure.

A heavy tension had settled over them. Levin cleared his throat. "So, what are you guys most looking forward to when you get home?"

"Do I have to say it?" Jeremy asked.

The brothers laughed.

He turned sideways in his seat. "Renee has been planning our wedding without me. We had to move the date. We were supposed to be married three weeks ago."

Levin glanced at him. "Oh, that sucks."

"It's okay. As long as I can be with her in the end, I'll be happy."

Completely understanding Jeremy's position, Levin laughed to himself. Years from now, this separation from Maggie would be a blur.

Jeremy looked towards the back seat. "What about you, Brent?"

"I'll f...f...finish the car I'm working on. And get b...b...back to work. I w...w...want to open my own sh...shop." He stared out the window, scowling.

"Is there some reason you can't do that?" Levin asked.

"I h...h...have to find sss...someone to talk to customers."

"I don't know about that." Following one of the vans, Levin drove into the oncoming lane to pass a slow truck. "If you do good work, that will speak for itself."

Brent grinned into the rear-view mirror.

"I think I want to move," Daniel said.

"Why?" Brent asked.

"I love my family, but not my city. There's a great medical school in Denver. I want to try to go there."

"Really?" Levin glanced into the back seat. "It would be nice to have you close by."

"Thanks. I need a change. What about you, Levin? Aside from the obvious, of course."

Levin laughed. "Yeah, getting Maggie back is job one." He tightened his grip on the wheel. "I just want to get back to normal, you know? Working. Visiting with my family. Dating Maggie. Going out with my friends. The way things were before Project Renovatio reared its ugly head."

He struggled to remember what life felt like six months ago, when he was a regular guy who generally lived a low-key existence, the way he liked it. Back then, he wasn't the product of a research organization that ultimately wanted to control him—or rather, that his half-brother would want him to join an army of super soldiers. There was no risk of public outcry against his very being, and he didn't have to stay away from the woman he loved for her own safety.

Six months ago, things were simple. Easy.

Shifting in his seat, he pushed the old life he longed for from his mind and tried to imagine his new one, the one he'd have after the encounter with Uriah's group. The one featuring him and Maggie and the life they'd build together.

****

Destiny leaned across the van's narrow aisle, towards Rana. "What do you think it will be like? You know, when we find them?" Her long, black hair was pulled into a ponytail, making her wide eyes seem brighter than usual against her tan skin.

Sitting backwards in the seat in front of Rana, Dante set down his book to answer his sister's question. "Hard to say. We don't know what their state of mind is." He moved his arrowhead across the backs of his fingers, like Rana had seen a guy at school do with a coin. "But I think we can assume that they're not stable, if they're trying to influence people outside of the Project."

"Yeah." Rana picked at her nails. "I'd say that's a pretty safe bet."

"I can't wait to get in there," Isaiah said. "Show them what we're made of." He punched his fist into his opposite palm. A few laughed.

Rana scowled at him. "Settle down, I don't want to have to stitch anyone together. We're not going to pick a fight." She tore a cuticle and winced, then sat on her hand to keep from damaging the skin further. "What did you train in, anyway?"

"I was in Dante's archery group."

"Really? Levin didn't say anything."

Isaiah shrugged. "He was pretty zoned out. Kept to himself. I wouldn't be surprised if he didn't know I was there."

"Yeah, but still." Rana didn't have a way to finish her thought. Her brother was usually attentive to those around him–or at least he had been before they arrived at the camp. Noticing one of their half-brothers had been training with him should have been automatic. Where was Levin's focus?

Liz's words returned to Rana in a flash–*He's so in love with her. He'll do anything to get to her.*

Dante's voice brought her mind back to the van. "He did work very hard, and he was only with us for two days. He practiced on his own in the evenings after that."

"That's true." Isaiah pulled a package of animal crackers from his backpack. "I don't think he was there when Dr. Craig showed us how to make bows to start fires."

"That was cool." Dante smiled. "I might practice doing that just for fun." He met Rana's eyes. "We'll have to show you sometime."

She scrunched her eyebrows at the odd suggestion. "All right." She shifted in her seat. "Why do we need to know that?"

Dante cleared his throat. "Part of the survivalist training." He slouched and held his book in front of his face, tapping his knee with the arrowhead.

Jason elbowed her from the neighboring seat. "Come on. Starting a fire with a bow could come in handy sometime. Even if you don't need it to survive."

"Why else would you do it."

"I dunno. To impress someone?" He raised his eyebrows.

She offered a polite laugh.

He turned sideways and leaned against the window. "So, arc you ready?"

"Ready for the battle we're driving into, or ready to be home?"

"How about both?"

She pulled her hand out from under her and started working on her hanging cuticle. "I'm not sure it will be a battle. Dr. Craig wouldn't have cut our training by two days if he thought we faced real danger." Inspecting the mess she'd made of three nails, she clasped her hands. "I'll just be happy when it's over and we can go home."

"He said we had to leave today or risk losing track of Uriah."

"Yeah." She looked up at him. "What about you? Are you ready?"

"I think so. Jeremy trained us well. I could probably roundhouse kick someone in the face if I had to."

She laughed.

"I miss how it was before," he said.

Oh, God. Why couldn't he figure out that dating her would be mind-numbingly awkward? *Oh, who am I taking to prom? Why, my sister's brother, of course. Who else?* "What do you mean?"

"Well . . ." He stared at his lap. "Before we knew about me and Dayla having the same Project father. You know . . . I really liked you." He met her eyes. "I still do."

She offered a polite grin. "Yeah, but there must be some laws against it. I mean, this sounds worse than dating cousins."

"I know, but it's not worse. We're not related."

Rana focused on her hands.

He broke the silence. "Sorry. I shouldn't have said anything."

No kidding. "It's okay. I kinda like what we have now."

He nodded and looked out the window.

Chapter Seven

With the group settled in the hotel ballroom, Levin found Dr. Craig sitting on a cot and taking off his shoes. After a short breath to settle his nerves, Levin coughed to get the old man's attention. "I need to run to a drugstore. I forgot some things."

Dr. Craig glanced up at him. "Like what? Your toothbrush? The front desk probably has extras."

A lump formed in Levin's throat. He should have sneaked out. No one would have noticed, but now Dr. Craig would definitely notice, having been informed of Levin's desire to leave. "Yeah, and some other stuff. I left one of my bags back at the camp."

Scowling, Dr. Craig scanned the room, focusing on the exit. "Find a 24-hour place. And choose a cot by the door so you don't wake anyone up when you get back."

"Okay." The knot in his stomach untied. He left the hotel and rushed to his car.

Levin didn't like lying, but he couldn't think of another way to get to Maggie tonight. He'd called her at the last gas stop to tell her he was coming over, thankful that few others knew about her. For a few minutes, Levin would pretend he lived a normal life.

Ten minutes later, he stood on the porch of Maggie's apartment, amazed he was there. Holding his breath, he knocked.

The door opened and there she stood, more beautiful than he remembered. Her jeans and purple V-neck shirt hugged her slender curves, and her brown hair perfectly framed her face. All of his memories of her came rushing back–the first time he saw her smile, how her eyes glowed in candlelight. She started crying and smiling at the same time. Happy tears. His heart beat so quickly he thought it would leap out of his body.

Storming inside, he pulled her close while shutting the door with his foot. She shook in his arms, and he squeezed her for a moment. He didn't have any words. For the first time in months, he was where he belonged, and he had to absorb every second.

"I've missed you so much." Her voice was so clear, so perfect.

He took her face in his hands and kissed her, the energy of it coursing through him and making him forget all the other worries that had taken hold of his mind during the previous weeks. He fixated on her soft lips against his. How had he managed to be away from them for so long?

When he finally released and connected with her deep brown eyes, they both laughed.

"I can't believe I'm here with you." He wiped her tears with his thumb.

She reached above his ear, brushing the strands with her fingers. "Your hair's getting long."

"Yeah." He smiled. "What do you think?"

"I like it." She didn't stop smiling either.

Unable to stop himself, he kissed her again, completely enraptured in the moment. His heart swelled with happiness. "God, I missed you." He pulled her close again, and they simply held each other. The sound of her gentle breathing told him all was right with the world.

They hadn't moved from their spot two feet from the doorway. He inhaled her clean scent and wished he could stay here with her. Pretending there was no Uriah or Project Renovatio, Levin was free to live how he wanted to live, to be with her simply because he could.

Finally pulling back, he let out a long breath. "I hate to say it, but I can't stay. Dr. Craig thinks I'm out buying toothpaste."

She connected with his eyes and took his hand. "Well, you'd better come here if we don't have much time. I have a present for you."

He raised his eyebrows. "Oh?"

Smiling, she led him into the living room, where she had a gift bag sitting on the end table. She picked it up, grasped the handles with both hands, and held it out to him. "I found this at the store the day after you texted me about fighting. I thought you'd appreciate it. I'm glad I can give it to you before anything happens."

Intrigued, he took the bag from her. He reached in, pulled out a black T-shirt, and unfolded it. A simple message flashed across the front in white capital block letters:

I DIDN'T COME HERE TO LOSE.

"Ha! This is great!"

"Try it on. I want to see how it looks on you."

He took off his T-shirt and had his arms in the sleeves of the new one when Maggie stopped him. "Oh my God! What happened to you?" She ran her finger along the pink scar that stretched from his left shoulder to his upper abdomen.

He watched her finger move across his skin. "I forgot you didn't know about that."

She stared at him with pleading eyes.

After tossing the shirt on the couch, he rubbed his neck. "It happened the night we got Mom back. When Scott revealed who he really was–I punched him in the jaw. He pulled out a knife, and . . ." He pursed his lips and gestured to the scar with his hand.

"You had stitches." She touched the smaller scars on either side of the big one.

"Yeah, Daniel–my brother–did that in the van on the way to the campsite."

Tears pooled in her eyes. "Why didn't you tell me?"

He held her in his arms. "I didn't want to worry you." Closing his eyes, he relished the feel of her hair on his bare chest before he pulled back. "Now, let's see how this looks."

He stepped away from her, grabbed the shirt and put it on, looked to the side, and puffed out his chest with his hands on his hips.

She laughed and wiped the tears from her face. "It's perfect."

"Thank you." He returned to her and gave her a quick kiss. "I love it. And I love you." He pulled her close for lingering kiss, moving his fingers into her hair. She inhaled and slid her hands under the front of his new shirt, making his pulse race.

He pulled back but kept his fingers in her hair. "I can't stay," he muttered in spite of his pounding heart, trying to remind himself more than her.

"I know." Without removing her hands from under of his shirt, she pulled him onto the couch.

****

The next morning, Rana and the forty-two other Project kids woke in the ballroom. They took turns showering in the few rooms the hotel opened for them. Two of Dr. Craig's workers distributed bagels and coffee to the ones who waited their turn.

Rana sat in a circle with Levin, her half-brothers, and a few other kids. Destiny spoke from across the circle. "Were you wearing that shirt last night? I love it! Where did you get it?" She directed her question towards Levin.

He glanced down at his shirt. "Oh, thanks. I found it at the store I went to last night." He looked at his lap and grinned.

Rana leaned towards him. "What's going on?"

"Nothing. I'm fine."

No, something was up. That spark that had been missing from his eyes the past few weeks was back. He was smiling again. She hadn't seen him look that way since . . . well, since he last saw Maggie.

She gasped at her realization. "Can we talk in the hall?"

His eyes narrowed. "Yeah. I guess."

They left the ballroom and stood next to a large window that overlooked the Colorado Front Range, facing each other. He crossed his arms.

Rana leaned towards him. "Did you see her last night?"

His eyes widened and he glanced around. Leaning close to her, he whispered through barely-open lips, "How could you possibly know that?"

She smiled. "You're acting like you did before. It's nice. You look happy. Did she give you the shirt?"

A wide grin took over his face. "Yeah."

"I like it. So, how is she?"

"She's . . . amazing." He stared at the floor past Rana and bit his lower lip.

He'll do anything to get to her.

Her mother's words echoed in her mind, but Rana couldn't have done anything about Levin's actions last night. "Okay. But you might want to tone it down a bit, or people will get suspicious. It only took me two sentences to figure it out."

He dramatically stretched his mouth out and forced it into a scowl.

She laughed and hit him on the arm.

****

Levin wanted to smack himself on the forehead for not changing out of the shirt. He'd returned to the hotel nearly three hours after he left and found everyone, including Dr. Craig, asleep. No one seemed to suspect he'd been gone more than half an hour, and it hadn't occurred to him that someone was paying enough attention to notice what he wore. If Dr. Craig or any of the drivers figured out he'd seen Maggie, they'd watch him so closely he wouldn't have a chance to see her again before they neutralized Uriah's group. Who knew how long that would take?

After last night, he became more resolute in his plan to see her as much as possible for as long as they were in Denver.

The others had believed his story about finding the shirt at the store, so he didn't worry they'd discover its true origin. He put on a different shirt after his shower, though, to limit any further questions.

When everyone finished showering, Dr. Craig stood on one side of the ballroom, obviously waiting for the noise to dissipate. The moment reminded Levin of the night they learned about Uriah.

Dr. Craig spoke when the room was quiet. "Good morning. I hope you all slept well. I have news that might hamper our efforts here, but we can work around it. Three inside contacts have been feeding me information on Uriah's group. They've all been sent to other cities in the past two days, so I don't have any current intelligence here. However, we can use the information they last gave me as a starting point."

Chatter filled the room. Maybe he didn't have as many people working for him as they all thought.

Pacing in front of them, the old man continued. "Today's mission is about surveillance. There are three locations we think are likely to house Uriah and his followers. All are abandoned buildings. The first is a warehouse, the second is a church, and the third is a small school.

"I want you to form three groups in these corners." He pointed to indicate the corners. "Each should have at least one person trained in first aid. I believe there are enough for two in each group." He looked at Daniel. "Is that right?"

"Yeah, there are six of us."

"Great." He turned back to the crowd. "I'd also like you to divide up by skills, just in case. It wouldn't make sense for all of our archers to be in one group. We have three vans with us, so each group will go to one of the places I mentioned and check it out. Keep weapons in the vans unless you're sure you need them. I don't expect you will today, though, because we just want to see what we're dealing with. Don't engage anyone with only a third of our whole group there. Tomorrow, when we know where they are, we'll form a new plan."

Levin paced behind the others. Why was engaging anyone part of Dr. Craig's directions? Weren't they going to use their numbers to intimidate? His silent fear that they would have to use the skills they'd been practicing crept into his chest again. He drummed his fingers against his leg.

"I can't stress this next point enough." He scanned the faces before him. "Do not attack unless you are attacked. Don't expect what we're doing to be like a battle you might have seen in a video game. Our goal is to stop Uriah's supporters, not kill the Project families he's influenced. They're misguided; they're not evil. We can probably still turn the more recent recruits. That said," he sighed, "if you feel you need to defend yourselves or your peers, do it. In fact, over the next few days, I would expect that to be the case. I want you to be mentally prepared for that outcome."

A girl in the middle of the room raised her hand. "I thought we were just making an appearance."

"Yes, I said that." He clasped his hands in front of him. "Since we arrived in Denver, I've received reports of Uriah's people beating family members of PR kids until they join with his cause. I wasn't aware of their . . ." he pressed his lips, "persuasive techniques. But that occurred in small settings, with individual families. Our numbers still may be enough to counter a larger gathering. The alternative is to go back to the camp, but Uriah's group will likely grow unchecked if we do that. This could be the only way to get you home safely." He shook his head. "I would hate to learn his followers used similar techniques on your families."

Silence filled the room. Levin imagined that like him, the others were questioning whether they would be ready to battle a violent faction after just over a week of training. Or maybe they were imagining their families being tortured.

"Okay, so go ahead and form your groups. Collect your bags and supplies, and load into the vans."

Chapter Eight

Levin stared past the driver and out the van's windshield as they headed to the warehouse. Familiar buildings rushed by, reminding him of his uncomfortable truth: he was home, but not really. They still had a job to do before he could really say he was home.

"Worried about something?" Daniel's question brought Levin's mind back to the van.

"Not really. Why?"

"You're fidgeting like crazy."

He stopped his bouncing leg and tapping finger. "Oh. I guess I am."

"So what's up?"

"Nothing. Just nervous about what we'll find."

Daniel shrugged. "I'm not sure today will be that interesting."

"I know. I just want to get this over with."

They rode for thirty minutes before arriving at the warehouse. There were no windows in the dingy, white exterior walls, and the only obvious access into the building was a single, foggy glass door. The metal loading bay doors appeared rusty and neglected, as did the dumpster sitting between them. Weeds grew from cracks in the pavement.

Levin eyed the structure for any inconspicuous windows or cameras. "How are we supposed to see what's going on inside?" If there was a group in there, they likely noticed the van and could be waiting to ambush them.

No one answered.

Dr. Craig broke the silence. "One of you can pretend you're driving around, lost, and looking for directions. It will have to be someone they won't recognize." He surveyed the van. "Amaya, will you do it? Take Travis with you."

"Sure. Be right back."

"Wait." Levin held out a hand. "That won't work. Who would stop at a place like this to ask for directions?"

"Maybe our car broke down." Amaya made her way to the door. "Who cares? They won't recognize us. They'll just think we're a couple of dumb kids."

Before Levin could argue further, Amaya and her brother left the van and entered the building through the unlocked glass door. Levin kept his eyes glued to the warehouse and strained to hear anything coming from inside. The place remained as silent and still as when they arrived.

Amaya and Travis returned minutes later; she shook her head as they reclaimed their seats. "There's only dirt and trash in there. We walked all around inside."

Dr. Craig scowled. "Let's catch up to the group going to the school."

As they traveled, Levin leaned forward and tapped the old man on the shoulder. "What are we doing here?"

He twisted around. "What do you mean?"

"You don't seem to know what's going on. I'd assumed you'd be on the van most likely to find these guys."

Dr. Craig glanced over Levin's shoulder, at the PRs filling the space behind him. "I'll talk to you about this privately when we get back to the hotel. It's more complicated than we thought, but broadcasting it won't help anyone."

Levin buried the urge to press the issue. Stressing the others about it wasn't the best option. He sat back in his seat.

****

Rana stared out the window, at the familiar buildings passing by. They were headed downtown, to the abandoned church, but she'd been in this area enough times to know where to find certain landmarks. It would be so easy to hop out of the van, get on a bus, and head for her house, as if she had no other reason to be in Denver than to simply live her life.

From the seat in front of her, Dante fussed with a stuck zipper on his backpack. Failing to fix it, he grunted and tossed the bag at his feet. "I don't like it."

"I'm sure we can get you another back–"

"That's not what I mean." He twisted around and met her eyes. "If these guys are in a church, then Uriah's not presenting himself as general-like, the way Scott did. It means he's presenting himself as

God-like." He kept his eyes on her for a few moments before staring out the window.

"I don't think that's why they'd hide in the church. Maybe the pews are a convenient place to sleep. Besides, we don't even know if anyone's there."

He clenched his jaw.

She leaned forward, resting her arms on the back of his seat. "Is there something else you're worried about?"

"Nothing specific." He sighed. "It's just . . . Scott wanted to turn us into an army, right? He tried to recruit directly, and when that didn't work, he lured us all into a large group." He focused out the window again. "This time, Uriah's doing what Scott started doing, only he's having more success. He can't beat every family into submission, so there must be more to it. Something different about his message or his mission."

Rana sat back, unsettled. Dante had a point–if people were quicker to join Uriah than they had been with Scott, then something was different this time. And they had no idea what it was.

Or did they? On the night Dr. Craig told them about Uriah, he'd said the PRs were hearing about their gifts for the first time. What would that be like? Rana had learned of her existence and gifts from her own mother in a matter-of-fact way; there was no suggestion that Rana should use her advantages for any greater purpose. What if she had learned about Project Renovatio from someone like Scott or Uriah? Could she have been persuaded to join with others like her?

The church appeared when the driver took them around a bend. Possibly as old as Colorado, the building showed obvious signs of neglect. Overgrown weeds met the tall, broken, stained-glass windows that ran along its length. A crumbling steeple graced its north side. The interior had to be huge. It would be ridiculous for Uriah's group to hide here, because it sat against a busy street–though maybe they thought it would be easier to blend in a big city.

"How are we gonna see what's inside?" Jason asked.

"I h…h…have an idea. D…drive up the street a little." Brent hopped out of the van.

Rana lunged toward the door as it slammed shut. "Brent, wait!"

He walked towards the church without looking back.

The driver pulled in front of the neighboring building. Rana watched Brent through the rear window, silently begging there was no one inside the church who would recognize him. He climbed the steps to the door and pulled, but it didn't open. He descended the steps and stood among the weeds, leaning beneath a broken window.

After fifteen minutes, Rana grew bored with watching him and sat forward in her seat. Why stay there so long if nothing was happening?

But maybe something was happening, something Brent could hear. He wouldn't stick around for no reason.

Rana twisted around again, watching Brent for any indication of activity inside. After several more minutes, Brent blocked his face with his hand and jogged to the sidewalk.

"D…d…drive." He climbed aboard and slammed the door behind him. When they were well down the road, he said, "Th…th…they're inside."

Rana's stomach knotted. "Are you sure?"

"Yeah. Th…th…the guy sss…said things like 'd…d…designed to b…b…be great'."

Brent's stammer had worsened, and sweat glistened on his brow.

"H…h…he even ssss…said sssss…" He grunted and slammed the side of his fist into the door.

Rana recoiled.

He took a breath. "He s…said sss…Scott's vision."

No wonder Brent had blocked his face when he returned to the van. His shorter hair and rounder face made him look less like Scott than Levin or Daniel did, but his appearance was similar enough that anyone who knew Scott could place him–and apparently, someone inside had known Scott well.

Rana swallowed the lump in her throat. "Brent, do you know who was talking?"

Keeping his eyes out the window, he shook his head.

"Could you tell why they were talking about it? They said that stuff in a conversation?"

"It ssss…sounded like a speech to nnn…nnn…" He sighed. "For followers."

"New followers?"

He nodded. "They sss…started moving when I came back."

Rana glanced out the rear window, but the church was out of sight.

"Do you think we can watch them somehow?" Jason asked.

"N...not without being ssss...seen."

"Okay, we're heading to the hotel," the driver said. "We'll meet up with everyone there and regroup."

****

Later that afternoon, everyone sat in the ballroom, and Rana told Dr. Craig what Brent had heard. She sat in the back of the crowd, waiting to learn what the discovery meant for all of them.

Dr. Craig reclaimed his spot at the side of the room. "Uriah's followers are working out of the abandoned church. Brent heard what sounded like a leader speaking to those going out to recruit PRs. The things he said are consistent with Scott's message, and he indicated that more people would be arriving tomorrow.

"I sent one of the drivers to the area to monitor the building. No one has come or gone in the hours since our van left. It's possible they're living at the church."

A boy near the front raised his hand. "Should we go back today?"

"No. We don't know where they are in the building unless the leader is talking, and that stopped shortly after Brent left. I'm stationing my people in shifts around the church to keep us posted about developments. For now, the plan is to go back tomorrow at the same time that the group arrived today. The speech sounded like an orientation for new arrivals, so it may be a daily occurrence."

"What are we gonna do when we get there?" Jason asked.

"Attempt diplomacy first. If there's an audience, we'll surround them–archers in the back, everyone else along the sides–and I'll talk to the leader about the original vision of PR. I'm not expecting he'll be receptive, but we want to appear as a formidable opposing force in case new PR families are there, those who were persuaded and think there is no way out. Remember, don't engage unless they do so first or if they threaten us. We'll capture the leader and try to convince the PR families to come with us."

"What if they don't turn, but they don't attack either?" Jeremy asked.

"We'll let them go."

Muttering moved through the crowd, and Rana held her breath. What was the point of all this, if the recruits could simply leave with a toxic message still in their minds? It would only be a matter of time before another Scott or another Uriah took charge.

Dr. Craig continued, "We can't force them to leave Uriah's group. If we did, we would be no better than they are. They get to choose, same as you. But I hope none of you are planning to join him."

Several in the room laughed.

"That said, if we remove the leader here and offer a new option, I believe the families will not choose to remain in the service of Uriah's group. They would have to give up everything to do so–their educations, their jobs . . . everything."

Rana huffed at the ironic statement. While not technically forced to stay at the camp, she and the others had to give up all those things in the name of safety, at least temporarily.

"Is Uriah the man Brent heard?" Destiny asked.

"I don't know. That will be my first question." He clasped his hands. "For your safety, you need to all stay here. One of the drivers is out buying board games right now." This elicited more chuckles. "We'll have food delivered in a few hours."

****

After dinner, Levin pulled Rana next to the big window outside the ballroom. "Can you do me a favor?"

"Okay. What?"

He glanced up and down the hall. "If anyone looks for me for the next hour, tell them I went for a walk around the hotel."

"What are you doing?" She glared at him.

He leaned towards her. "I'm meeting Maggie at a park down the street."

Her eyes widened. "Are you sure that's a good idea? What if Uriah's people are watching? We know for sure they're in Denver now."

"If they were watching, wouldn't they have come for us here?"

She racked her mind for reasons Levin should stay, and all she could come up with was the potential spying bad guys. Dr. Craig had been vague in his reasons for keeping them there, so she didn't have anything to fall back on.

He'll do anything to get to her.

She put her hand on his arm. "Why don't you talk to Dr. Craig first? Find out why he doesn't want anyone to leave."

He shook his head. "If I do that, he'll make sure I stay. It's fine. Trust me. Let me be a grown-up for one night."

She gritted her teeth. Maybe he was right. If Uriah's followers knew where they were and cared enough to follow Levin, they would have likely confronted Dr. Craig's group by now. "Fine. But don't be too long."

He smiled and squeezed her shoulder. "Thanks." He took off down the hall.

She returned to her game of Balderdash, pretending all was well. Her gut told her she should chase Levin down and convince him to stay at the hotel, but she'd already told him she'd cover for him. He was her big brother, and she'd always trusted him to know what was best for them. She wished she could trust him now.

****

The sun had nearly set when Levin arrived at the park. Maggie sat with her legs crossed on a bench, watching the other people and laughing at a toddler chasing a bird. Levin stood and gazed at her for a minute before she locked eyes with him.

She stood as he rushed to her. Wrapping her in his arms, he pressed his lips into hers.

"Well, hello to you too!"

He laughed. "Sorry. Making up for lost time."

Taking her hand, he led her down the cement path. The pleasant day had given way to a cool evening; she wore jeans and a sweater. He was still dressed for the day, and before long, the brisk air cut through his T-shirt. For warmth, he put his other hand in his pocket, feeling Dayla's note. He smiled when he remembered what she'd written.

Maggie ran her fingers up and down his arm. "Are you cold?"

"A little. I don't mind." He gazed into her eyes as his foot caught a raised section in the sidewalk. He let go of her hand and took three huge steps to avoid falling. Heat rushed to his face. "Wow. Smooth."

Maggie smacked her hand over her mouth and giggled.

"I'm glad my clumsiness is so amusing." He returned to her and kissed her again, then pulled back and exhaled a long breath, pretending they could spend the entire evening together and that he didn't have a reason to leave her.

When they resumed walking, he weaved his fingers between hers as she asked the questions she must have had the night before, or perhaps since he'd texted her from the camp.

"Who are you fighting? And when?"

"There's a radical offshoot of Project Renovatio that wants to force PR kids into an army and dominate society."

She snickered.

"I know. It sounds ridiculous. But they bully people into joining their cause, and they could pose a threat to our families if they're left unchecked. We want to take out the leader so the faction will fall apart."

"And how will you do that?"

"I'm not sure. They're at an old church. We're going to face them tomorrow." He buried the wince caused by his weak answer.

She pulled on his arm, stopping them from walking. "Will it be dangerous?"

"It might. But we have a big group. I think we'll be okay. Ignoring the other group will be worse, in the end." He grinned as he tried to sound as reassuring as possible.

They walked in silence for a minute before she spoke again. "Do you guys have the means to fight another group?"

He nodded. "We've been training."

"Training? In what?"

"Different things. I've been doing Taekwondo and archery."

"Really? I'd love to see that."

"Which one?"

Her eyes narrowed. "Yes."

He laughed.

She froze in her tracks. "Did I miss your birthday?"

"Yeah. It sucked."

"Sorry." She pulled him close, and he held her in his arms, feeling her warmth against him. "I'll have to think of some way to make it up to you."

"Well, you already gave me a shirt, but if you insist, I'm not going to argue with you." He winked.

She pulled away and grinned. "Behave yourself."

"That's no fun." He picked her up by her waist and spun her around. She yelled and laughed as she reached for his shoulders.

"I missed that sound so much." He lowered her to the ground, put his hand on the back of her neck, and brought her close for a deep kiss. He tried to memorize her soft lips as they moved across his, not caring if anyone saw them. When he pulled back, he rested his forehead against hers. "I don't want to be away from you again."

"I know. You'll be home soon–"

"No, you don't understand what I'm saying." He stood straight and stroked her hair. Though he'd thought about it constantly the past few days, he hadn't planned on bringing it up tonight, and his nerves nearly stopped him from doing it. But gazing into her eyes, he knew this was the right thing. "Being away from you doesn't make sense, and I don't want to do that anymore. I'm a better man when I'm with you. Just ask Rana."

She giggled.

He put his hand on her cheek. "I've thought about this a lot. I can't imagine life without you. When this is over, I want you to be my wife."

She reached up and put her hands on either side of his head, pulling him towards her. She kissed him so intensely he considered scooping her up and running to her apartment with her.

When she pulled back, she kept her face inches from his. "I was wondering when you'd ask."

He took that as a yes.

****

"Dr. Craig? Can I talk to you?" Rana wrung her hands, second guessing her decision even as she stood here.

He peered over the top of his book and sat up on his cot. "Of course. What do you need?"

"Can we go into the hall?" She swallowed, trying to remind herself of Levin's argument–Uriah not finding them likely meant he didn't know they were here. Levin would visit Maggie and return with no problems. But the simple fact that Uriah had followers in the city was enough to worry her to the point of distraction–what if Levin was wrong, and now he was in danger?

Dr. Craig set his book on the cot. "Sure."

She stopped by the window and faced him. "Levin left. He went to see his girlfriend."

"What?" Dr. Craig leaned towards her, then looked out the window while clenching his jaw. "Do you know where he went? It's important we get him back here before someone sees him."

"Is he in danger?"

"We all are. Where is he?"

She glanced out the window. "Um . . . he said he was going to a park, but I don't know where. I think he walked, though. So it must be close."

Dr. Craig walked to the ballroom doorway and peered inside. "Eric. Come here."

The driver joined them in the hall, and Dr. Craig explained the situation. "I want you to take Rana and look for him. Use the GPS to find parks in the area." He faced Rana. "Sit in the back of the van, behind the tinted windows."

She followed Eric to the van, where he used the GPS to locate parks. She tried to keep her mind off whatever danger Dr. Craig was talking about.

They found Levin with Maggie in the second park they searched. Eric stopped on the street, but they were difficult to see in the waning daylight.

"Should we go get him?" she asked as Levin picked up Maggie and spun her around.

He looked so happy, and he would soon know she ratted him out. The knot in her stomach tightened. Nothing was going to happen. She shouldn't have said anything.

"I don't think so. It's almost dark. If he doesn't leave in ten minutes, I'll go get him. Better to not draw attention to ourselves, in case someone's watching." Eric kept his focus on the park.

She stared out the window. Levin was talking to Maggie now. "What did Dr. Craig mean we're all in danger?"

"Uriah's group is more ruthless than we originally thought, but many of them are in San Diego now. Dr. Craig didn't want to scare you unnecessarily. I asked him today if we should take you all back to the camp instead of following them."

"What did he say?"

"He wants to see what we find tomorrow. Going back to the camp means you'll be there indefinitely. This is likely our only chance to take Uriah out of power. If we wait, he may have so many followers he'll be unstoppable."

She swallowed her anxiety and returned her attention to the park. Levin and Maggie were kissing, and Rana looked away when it went on long enough that watching them officially became awkward.

A few minutes later, Levin and Maggie walked in opposite directions. Levin kept a brisk pace towards the hotel, beaming the whole way.

"What about now? Can we pull up next to him?" she asked. Levin walked quickly, almost jogging.

"No. He'll be back shortly."

Chapter Nine

Dr. Craig met Levin at the doorway to the ballroom. "Would you mind telling me where you were?"

"Uh . . . I went for a walk."

"Rana talked to me. Would you like to try again?"

Levin's jaw dropped. "What?" He glanced past the man and into the room.

Dr. Craig leaned into his line of sight. "She's not here. I sent her with Eric to go look for you. It would be nice if you told me the truth."

Levin scowled. "I met my girlfriend at a park." How could Rana rat him out?

"Wait here." He entered the room and re-appeared a minute later holding a large envelope. "I want to show you something. Let's go into the ballroom next door. It's empty."

Levin silently followed.

He snapped around when he heard his sister's voice behind him. "There he is." She walked with Eric down the hall.

He stormed over to her. "You told on me? Like I'm a child?" Standing in place, he leaned towards her while tightening his fist and glaring.

"I couldn't let you–"

"Let me do what? Behave like a normal person for a change? You don't get to decide that for me!"

She stared at him.

"Come on." The old man's voice called him back to the other room.

Levin pointed at Rana. "I'll talk to you later."

They entered the empty ballroom, and Dr. Craig unstacked two chairs.

"If you're going to scold me, just get on with it. I don't need a heart-to-heart." Levin crossed his arms.

"I'm not your father, Levin. I'm not here to scold you. I need to show you something." He gestured to one of the chairs. "Have a seat."

Levin nervously bounced his leg, then turned his chair so it was angled away from the old man.

Dr. Craig opened the envelope, pulled some pictures from it, and handed them to Levin. "I received these after we arrived last night. They're photos showing the people Uriah's people brutalized."

Levin flipped through the pictures as the anger in his gut gave way to horror: the first pictures showed bruised wrists and ankles, then a neck with a dark rope burn around it.

He swallowed and willed himself to keep looking at the pictures, which grew steadily worse. After a stab wound that had exposed the contents of an abdomen, there was a gunshot wound that had destroyed a leg.

Breathless and nauseated, Levin focused on the last picture. His heart pounded as he inferred the purpose of this meeting. Dr. Craig hadn't planned to simply reprimand him.

"These aren't PR kids. They are family members of PR kids. The one showing ligature marks around the neck died."

"Why are you showing me these?" Levin thrust the photographs back at their supposed leader.

Putting his elbows on his knees and leaning into them, Dr. Craig closed some of the distance between him and Levin. "You need to know what the group is capable of. By going to visit your girlfriend out in public like that, you've put her and all of us at risk." His tone was firm but not angry. He glanced at the floor. "You look just like Scott. If someone in his group was paying attention and recognized you, they now know who she is and where we are."

Levin pressed his lips, and it took a minute before he found words again. His voice cracked. "Do you think these people are watching that closely?"

"I have no idea. We know they're concentrated in this area. Or they were."

Levin sat in silence for a moment. "You should have told us about this."

Dr. Craig nodded. "Levin, I'm a geneticist, not a general. I'm trying to figure out how much you all need to know as we go along."

"But what if we don't want to face these guys?" Levin stood. "Don't we at least deserve the choice? You didn't know they were dangerous before, but you know now!" He paced, rubbing the back of his neck with his hand as worry about Maggie consumed him.

Dr. Craig stood. "You have a choice. Stand up to Uriah or go back to the camp. But if you go home, you're in danger, and so is anyone who associates with you, including your girlfriend. I promise you that. Go back to the camp, and you could be there for years. We don't have to face Uriah's group, but if we leave, they will only get stronger." He lowered his hands, and he strained his jaw as he focused on the wall. Tears pooled in his eyes.

He was crying?

Dr. Craig wiped his eyes with his finger. "The kids expect me to be a leader, but our information always seems to be a step behind." He cleared his throat. "Scott's the reason you can't go home, and I feel responsible for that, since I didn't stop him at the beginning."

Levin tried to swallow the lump in his throat, recalling how less than six months earlier, Scott had duped him and his other half-brothers into believing Dr. Craig was against them. Learning about their genetic gifts and their prescribed reasons for existence had clouded Levin's judgement. Had he paid more attention, he might have seen Scott for what he was and kept him from gathering all the Project Renovatio kids together, trapping them and trying to brainwash them with ideas of designed superiority.

Of course, if Levin had kept that from happening, Scott would still be in charge, maybe with Uriah as a right-hand man, and there would be no group to oppose them.

Funny how things work out.

As if someone flipped a switch, Dr. Craig turned his attention to the chairs and stacked them, showing no further sign of emotion. "I'm having my guys take turns guarding the ballroom through the night, in case someone saw you. I think it would be nice if you took a shift."

Levin stared at the floor. Somehow, Dr. Craig could tell him he had a choice while making him feel cornered at the same time. "Sure."

As Dr. Craig headed for the door, Levin stopped him. "Would Maggie be safer if we brought her here?"

He nodded. "I think so. Give Eric her address, so he can pick her up."

Relief covered Levin for the first time since the conversation started.

They rejoined the group in the ballroom, and Levin looked up Maggie's address on his phone, passing it along to Eric. He then lay on his cot, put his hand behind his head, and stared at the ceiling.

Maggie would soon be here with him. The thought made him smile, until the follow-up thought took it away.

Maybe here with him wasn't a safe place for her to be.

****

Levin rushed to the ballroom's doorway, where Eric was waving him over. He tried to peer around Eric to see Maggie in the hall.

"I waited an hour." Eric pursed his lips. "She didn't go home."

"What?" Levin ran his hand over his hair. "That doesn't make sense." He closed his eyes, trying to imagine where she could be. "Will you try again?"

"Sure. We'll give her a couple of hours. She might be out with friends. I'll let you know." He walked past Levin and entered the ballroom.

Levin stood silently. Wouldn't Maggie have said something if she had plans after their meeting?

He returned to the ballroom, grabbed his keys from his backpack, and re-entered the hall.

As he reached the turn towards the main entrance, a tug on the back of his arm stopped him.

"Going somewhere?" Dr. Craig asked.

Levin turned and pressed his lips. "I need to look for her. I know the places she likes to go."

Dr. Craig shook his head. "Absolutely not. If anyone saw you before, they'll be looking–"

"I have to do something!"

Dr. Craig glared at him. "I get that you want to protect her. But putting yourself and the group in more danger isn't the way to do that. Eric told me he'll go back to her place tonight. But I can't let you leave. I'll take your car keys if I have to."

"Are you gonna ground me, too?" Levin clenched his jaw.

Dr. Craig took a step back. "What shift are you taking?"

"What?"

"To keep watch over your siblings and friends, to make sure no one dangerous gets to them. What shift?"

Levin scowled. "Four AM 'til dawn." He squeezed his keys in his fist until they painfully dug into his palm.

"Good." Dr. Craig returned to the ballroom.

Levin stood in place, running his fingers along the edge of his car key.

"Dammit." He rushed to his cot, put his keys into his backpack, and sent Maggie a text. He turned his silent phone in his hand for a few minutes before sliding it into his pocket. It wasn't like her to leave a text unanswered.

If Maggie were here with him, at least he would know where she was. The images of Dr. Craig's photographs flashed in his mind, and he squeezed his eyes closed, forcing himself to focus instead on his memories of the park.

Thirty minutes later, Maggie still hadn't answered his text, and everyone in the room had settled into their cots and bedrolls. Levin didn't try to sleep. He stared at the dark ceiling and considered how his impatience might have cost him the best thing in his life.

Someone tapped him on the arm later into the night. After twisting around to see who it was, he took his phone out of his shoe and checked the time. 12:14.

Eric whispered near his ear. "I went back to her place. She still wasn't there. Could she have stayed somewhere else?"

"I don't think so." She didn't stay with friends, so the only other place she could be staying was . . .

No. He refused to believe Maggie was staying with another man, especially after she'd agreed to marry him just a few hours ago.

"I'm not going back tonight. I'll check again in the morning. I'm sure she'll turn up," Eric said.

"Okay."

Levin rested his head on his pillow and resumed his cycle of torturous thoughts until it was time for his four AM watch shift.

****

Shortly after she woke, Rana found her brother standing in the hall. He leaned against the wall with his hands in his pockets, facing the window. Last night, he'd told her someone was going to pick up Maggie, but Rana hadn't seen her. That was before Dr. Craig showed the photographs to her and the rest of the group.

She stepped up next to him. "How's it going?"

He responded without looking away from the window. "She never made it home last night. Eric said he checked again an hour ago."

She leaned towards him. "Maybe she stayed somewhere else. Does she visit her parents?"

"Not overnight. They live twenty minutes away." He glanced at his feet and took a long breath. He finally faced her; his red eyes told of a stressful night.

"What do you think happened?"

"I think one of Uriah's guys followed her from the park and took her. Or," his voice caught. He closed his eyes and swallowed. "Or they did something to her and left her there."

She weighed the possibilities. "I don't think that's it. If they did something to her, they lose their

leverage with you. If they took her, we'll find her."
She put her hand on his arm until he looked at her.
"Okay? We'll find her. We all have gifted
intelligence, right?" She offered an awkward smile,
then hugged him. He squeezed her tighter than he
ever had.

Keep an eye on him.

He coughed, pulled back, and held her shoulders.
"I want you to go back to the camp. Find some others
who want to go, enough to fill a van."

Her jaw dropped. "I can't do that."

"Didn't Dr. Craig say you had a choice to stay or
go back?"

"Yeah, but–"

"Then go. Maggie's already in danger. There's
no reason for you to be."

Rana swallowed. Their situation had grown
significantly more dangerous in the past twenty-four
hours, but it was like Levin said in the beginning–if
they had a chance of winning and going home in
safety, they needed as many people on their side as
possible. "Staying with this group is the only way
we'll get home. And I want to go home."

Chapter Ten

Levin was among the first to take a shower after his shift. He dressed in his last clean pair of jeans and the shirt Maggie gave him, not caring if anyone figured out how he got it. He remembered to move Dayla's note from his other pants; it was the only thing that provided a respite from his worry, however brief.

He joined the group in the ballroom for breakfast, but his anxiety crowded out his appetite. Hoping that having something in his stomach might calm his nerves, he nibbled on dry cereal, but it tasted funny. Those talking around him were incomprehensible. Everything had an awkward quality to it, like it was all out of tune with the rest of the universe.

Dr. Craig clapped his hands twice as he made his way to the side of the room, and the ambient chatter died off. Time for the morning announcement.

"Forty people have left the church, and a few have entered. We don't know how many are still inside, but they don't appear to have anyone on guard. The driver I sent can get close enough to hear movement and talking. Our plan is the same as the one I described yesterday, assuming we hear the speaker the way Brent did. We're leaving in ten minutes, so start heading to the vans."

As everyone funneled out of the room, Levin weaved his way around the others to reach Dante. "Did you bring all the bows?"

"I brought some of the extra ones. I don't know if the one you were using is among them. Come, have a look." Dante led Levin to one of the vans parked at the far end of the lot. He opened the back, and Levin inspected the cargo.

"I see it." Levin picked up his bow and a quiver of arrows.

Dante rested his hand on Levin's shoulder. "I'm glad you're here. We need you."

Levin suppressed a laugh. If Dante knew how Levin had endangered them all, he wouldn't be so glad.

****

At the church, they piled out of the vans and stood together on the sidewalk. Avoiding attention was difficult in the bright daylight, so instead of trying to hide the weapons, they walked around as if weapons were normal accessories and agreed to tell anyone who asked that they were practicing a war re-enactment. Aside from a few lingering glances from passing motorists, no one seemed concerned with their presence.

Levin placed himself in the middle of the crowd. His appearance was so similar to Scott's–Rana had thought a photograph of Scott was really of Levin the first time she saw it–that anyone who'd worked with

Scott would easily place their group. Levin and his half-brothers could give them away just by being there.

He shook his leg as cars passed; if any bystanders grew suspicious and called the cops, any hope of stopping Uriah here–and of rescuing Maggie, if she was here–would be lost.

Dr. Craig told them to wait while he tried the door. As he reached the bottom of the steps, a tall, young man wearing a green Izod shirt and tan slacks emerged from the building.

"Levin Davis!" Izod called out.

Levin's jaw dropped. He quickly closed his mouth but hoped those surrounding him concealed the shock on his face–these people knowing his name and calling him out directly could only mean trouble.

"Levin Davis!" the man repeated. "Which one of you is Levin Davis?"

Dr. Craig put a foot on the bottom step. "Who wants to know?"

The man looked down at him. "There's someone here who wishes to see him. Alone. But if he's not interested, we can dispose of her."

Oh, God. Levin pushed his way to the front of the group and resisted the urge to rush up the steps and tackle the guy. He could be the key to getting Maggie back.

"You must be Levin." Izod studied him. "You look just like Scott."

"Where is she?"

"Inside. You won't need those." He pointed to Levin's bow and arrows.

"What if I bring them anyway?"

"You won't see her."

Levin handed his weapon to Jeremy.

He rushed to the stairs, his pounding heart echoing in his ears as he tried to imagine what he might find inside. As he set his foot on the first step, pressure on his shoulders kept him from ascending.

Dr. Craig held him in place, leaned close to his ear, and whispered, "They don't hurt PR kids. If you can, fight them. If you're not back in five minutes, we'll assume you were captured and break down the door to come get you."

"Okay." Levin climbed the steps.

Before leading Levin inside, the man addressed the group. "You all stay out here. If you enter, Levin won't have to worry about the girl anymore."

Levin stared at Dr. Craig with wide eyes and raised brows, hoping Dr. Craig understood not to come after him in five minutes.

Izod led Levin into the church and locked the door behind them. They walked across a dusty foyer and past an empty sanctuary. Where was everyone?

Levin followed the man down a flight of creaky stairs to a dimly lit basement. The small room at the bottom was empty except for Maggie, tied to a chair in the far corner.

She looked at him and immediately cried; her tears soaked into the bandana that gagged her. She wore the same loose sweater and jeans as the night before.

"Maggie!" He took a step towards her. Izod grabbed his right arm at the same moment a burly black-haired guy–he must have been behind the propped-open door–grabbed his left, stopping his rush to her. He pulled against them as an older, bald man wearing glasses emerged from a hallway.

"So what she says is true. You did come for her."

Levin stopped struggling. "I know you. You were with Scott that night. Peter."

"You have a good memory."

"What do you want? Where's Uriah?"

Peter took a step towards Levin but still maintained a respectable distance. "Scott was your brother."

"You didn't answer my question."

"Let me finish. Surely, Scott told you his plan. I wonder, was any part of it . . . appealing to you?"

"Scott didn't tell me anything. And even if he had, I wouldn't be on his side. He was delusional."

"Are you sure?" He looked at Maggie. "She's lovely, but she's . . . average. You were made for so much more."

Levin strained against the men holding him. If he could just get one of them to loosen their grip a little . . .

Peter shook his head. "It's a shame you don't know your station, Levin. You're supposed to rule. All that about just being able to survive is a crock. Dr. Craig wants to deny you your place because the government is paying him to keep you down."

Levin glared at Peter. A foul taste collected in the back of his throat.

"That's fine. You don't have to say anything. But I can't help but realize what a fine soldier you would be. If you share Scott's gifts," he walked closer to Levin and said in a loud whisper, "you could even take charge over Uriah."

"I don't want what you want. Let her go."

"I think I can change your mind." Peter stepped away, stood next to Maggie, pulled a small gun from his pocket, and pointed it at her head.

"No!" Levin said through clenched teeth.

"Join me."

Levin's rage took over. He yanked his arm away and smashed Izod's face with a back fist. Whipping around, Levin punched Burly in the nose, crunching it. Burly brought both hands to his face. Levin kicked him into the wall.

Lunging, Levin hoped to cover the distance between himself and Peter before –

"Stop!" Peter pointed the gun at Levin's eye. He directed his next order to the battered men standing by the door. "Leave."

As they stumbled away, Peter focused on Levin. "Do you love her?" His tone was casual, as if he were having a friendly conversation. "Maybe you shouldn't let her watch you die."

"You won't shoot me. You don't hurt PRs." Levin stared at the gun and silently begged his heart to stop pounding. The sound of Maggie's terrified gasps permeated the otherwise silent room.

Peter eyed Levin over the gun. "You know, I often wonder if Scott would still be alive if you hadn't jumped on the stage that night."

"I didn't kill him," Levin said, sensing Peter's line of reasoning. "*He* stabbed *me*."

"Oh, I remember. But really, everything that happened was because of you. Your mother wouldn't have been there to shoot Scott if she hadn't tried to break communication with the Project."

"You're not the Project. And Scott kidnapped my mother. He's the reason she was there."

Loud thuds came from upstairs. His group was trying to get in. He was out of time.

Peter scowled. "No. This is your last chance. Join me." His gun-holding arm had slumped a bit, and he straightened it to level the barrel with Levin's face.

Levin concentrated on the gun. He had to knock it away from Peter. As he pulled his arm back, Peter turned it towards Maggie and fired.

"No!"

The bang echoing through the room smothered Levin's scream. He rushed to her and fell to his knees.

She slumped over, blood streaming through her hair from the wound on the opposite side of her head. The bullet had gone clean through.

Panting, he reached for her, his love, now still and lifeless.

He shook his head and stood, staring at her. "No. This . . ." Motion in the corner of his eye caught his attention.

Peter was pointing the gun at him.

His heart pounded, and before he could think, he yelled and kicked Peter in the chest. Peter stumbled backwards. A second kick struck Peter in the head. He fell to the floor and dropped the gun. Levin jumped on his chest and pummeled his face with all his strength, throwing punches faster than should have been possible. Bones crunched under his fist over and over again. Blood splattered on his face. The world closed around him, his focus centering on the murderer.

Someone grabbed Levin's arms, holding them up in a forced surrender. "Levin, stop."

Levin wrenched his hand away and punched again.

"No, stop!" Dr. Craig fell onto Levin's back and grabbed his wrist. "You have to stop!"

Levin took a few breaths before releasing the tension against Dr. Craig hands. He stared at Peter's mangled face before the realization hit him. "Maggie."

He stumbled sideways and over himself to get to her and wrapped her in his arms, but he couldn't lift her while she was tied to the chair. Kneeling behind her, he fumbled with the restraints. "You have to help me! We have to get her out of here!"

Dr. Craig stood next to the chair and put his fingers on Maggie's neck. "Levin, she's gone."

Levin couldn't make his hands work to untie the knots.

"We have to go. Right now." He crouched next to Levin.

"I can't leave her here!" Levin didn't look away from the ropes.

Dr. Craig put a hand on Levin's shoulder.

"Don't touch me!" Levin shot to his feet. "Why aren't you helping me? What's wrong with you?" He stepped back a few paces then returned to the ropes on the other side of the chair.

Dr. Craig met him there, leaning close. "Levin, listen! Rana and the others need you outside with them, before the cops or anyone else gets here." He closed his eyes. "I know you want to do something. You can't help Maggie now, but you can help them.

They need you. We've already been here too long."
He stood. "I'll make sure someone takes care of
Maggie."

Levin glared at the man and swallowed. What
was happening? This couldn't be real.

Levin, she's gone.

He looked at his shaking hands and dropped the
ropes. Blood had pooled on the floor–her blood. His
fiancée's blood. How could he leave her here?

He ran around the chair, framed her face in his
hands, and gazed into her eyes.

Dr. Craig was right. She was gone.

Rana needs you.

A sob escaped, and against everything he wanted
to do, he stood. Dr. Craig put his arm around Levin's
shoulders, leading him towards the door. As they left
the basement, Levin looked back to her one last time.

They reached the top of the stairs, where Jeremy
stood over the two unconscious bodies of the men
who had held Levin's arms minutes earlier.

Levin's stomach rebelled, and acid burned his
throat. He rushed out the door and down the steps.

****

Rana picked at her nails as she watched Dr. Craig
and Jeremy break open the door and rush inside,
resisting the urge to run after them. Dr. Craig had
instructed the rest of the group to wait on the
sidewalk.

A loud bang came from the building.

Her pulse cranked up. "Was that a gunshot?"
With her eyes glued to the door, she pushed her way
past the others.

Destiny grabbed her arm. "What are you doing? You can't go in there."

"What if they shot him?" Rana pulled her arm away.

"If they did and you go in there, they'll shoot you."

"But . . ." She stretched up on her tiptoes, as if she could see through the high windows that way. "There was only one shot. Dr. Craig and Jeremy have been in there a while."

"Maybe they were captured."

Rana snapped around. "And what if they were? We go in and fight for them, right?" Her gut knotted. As the words left her mouth, the reality of their situation hit her: they weren't going to make an appearance. They would surely have to fight. It had already started, and they were all waiting outside. "We need to get in there. All of us."

As she stepped towards the door again, Levin bolted out. At the bottom of the steps, he collapsed to his knees and threw up.

"What?" Rana ran for him, but halfway there, Dr. Craig grabbed her shoulders and stopped her. Jeremy appeared behind him, silently crying. He stared at Levin with pure anguish covering his face.

Whatever fight had occurred was apparently over. And they were on the losing end.

Her eyes darted from Jeremy to Levin and back again. "What happened?"

Levin put his bloody hands in his hair and screamed through his teeth.

"Tell me!" Rana yanked away from Dr. Craig's grasp and ran to her brother, stopping in her tracks several feet away.

Blood covered his hands and arms, so much that only a severe injury could be responsible. Yet he didn't have any obvious wounds, and no one treated him like he was injured.

Whose blood was it?

Possibilities flashed in her mind. Only one person was still unaccounted for. "Was Maggie in there?"

Dr. Craig stared at her, then directed his attention to the group. "Everyone back in the vans, quickly." Taking her arm, he pulled her away from the others and bent over, placing his face inches from hers. "Peter killed Maggie in front of him."

"Oh my God!" Rana put her hand over her mouth.

Dr. Craig went to the others, hustling them into the vehicles.

She stood in place, begging reality to be different, until she and Levin were the only Project kids still outside. Her brother, who had acted as a father to her as she grew, was frozen on the sidewalk. Paralyzed by what he must have seen.

No one stood between them now. She could run to him and look into his eyes. Let him know she was still there.

But she stayed in place, helpless. Her chance to help him had come and gone at the hotel last night, when she let him leave. Because she'd done that, this was his new reality.

Dr. Craig approached her. "Help me get him into the van."

They stood on opposite sides of Levin's kneeling form. His back moved up and down with slow breaths–if not for those, he could have passed for a statue. He hadn't even moved away from where he'd gotten sick.

A lump formed in her throat. Whatever happened was likely repeating in his head, so nothing else would matter. Piecing together what she knew–a gunshot, blood, and death–she could only imagine what his mind was making him see. *Why didn't I keep him from leaving?*

The old man crouched. "Levin, we have to leave now." He faced Rana, "Put your arm around his back."

She did, and they lifted her brother to his feet. Levin shook them away and walked by himself.

They boarded the last van, which now seated all of her half-brothers. Levin sat alone in the seat behind the driver, putting his elbows on his knees and his hands in his hair. Wishing she knew how to help him, she claimed the seat next to him so he would know he wasn't alone.

Chapter Eleven

Levin had wanted to stay on the sidewalk until it swallowed him. He had a vague recollection of Dr. Craig and Rana helping him up and walking to the van, but everything was a foggy memory, like the last remnants of a nightmare.

After a silent ride to the hotel, he entered the empty ballroom. No one followed him.

He sat on the floor in the corner farthest from the door, rested his elbows on his knees and his head in hands, and stared into the space, listening to the silence.

Images of Maggie flashed through his mind in an endless loop: her shiny brown hair, her smile, her laugh.

The blood.

He lowered his hands, squeezed his eyes closed, and laid his head back into the corner. Taking deep breaths, he tried to control the anger coursing through his body. When the pain became too great, he jumped to his feet.

He stormed across the room to a shiny, black trash can. Lifting it above his head, he screamed as he threw it. The crash echoed through the space as he ran to it and kicked it repeatedly, grunting with each impact.

By the time he stopped, he was shaking and panting as he stared at the dented cylinder. Collapsing to his knees, he dug his nails into his scalp. "Why didn't I stop him?" He folded himself in half and wept, his tears soaking into his jeans. "I'm sorry."

Something else registered in his brain: pain. His hands hurt.

They shook as he pulled them away from his hair. Blood covered them. Peter's blood.

He had to wash it off.

He rushed to the bathroom, hoping no one would see him. Daniel stood by the sink, drying his hands. Why couldn't everyone disappear?

Daniel stood by as Levin washed off the murderer's blood and watched it swirl down the drain. It took four applications of soap to remove all of it, revealing the damage he'd done. The back of his right hand was swollen, and he couldn't bend three of his fingers without intense pain.

"Mind if I take a look?" Daniel asked. Stepping closer, he took Levin's hand in his and pressed the swollen places. Levin winced.

"I think you broke these bones." Daniel pointed behind the knuckles of his index, middle, and ring fingers. "I can take care of it. Come on."

Daniel led Levin to the ballroom where their peers sat around and talked. Several glanced at them but looked away just as quickly.

"Sit on your cot. I'll be right back," Daniel said.

Levin sat and focused on the floor.

Did they know everything from last night until now happened because of his choices? He closed his eyes in an attempt to hold his emotions in check and swallowed in spite of his dry mouth.

"Let's go next door. It's more private."

Levin opened his eyes. Daniel stood above him, holding a first-aid kit.

They entered the room and stepped over the garbage that cluttered the floor. Daniel looked at the damaged can. "What . . ." He shook his head as if realizing his question wouldn't be answered.

Levin lifted his hand up, and Daniel poked around the knuckles some more. "Best I can tell without an x-ray, you cracked the bones, so I'm just going to wrap it. You have to keep these fingers immobilized until they're healed, okay?"

Levin nodded.

Daniel started to wrap Levin's hand and fingers. "Do you want to talk about it?"

Levin closed his eyes. "Just wrap it, okay?" He covered his face with his free hand as a few tears escaped. Daniel kept his attention on his task. When he finished, he patted Levin on the shoulder and left him alone in the room.

Leaning against the wall and sliding to a sitting position, Levin forced himself to pretend this was all a nightmare and he would soon wake up. Maggie was still alive, waiting for him at her place.

The agony in his hand brought him back to reality. He pulled off his shirt and lay on the floor, using the shirt as a pillow. Maggie had touched this, run her hands under it to feel his skin. He buried his face in the cotton, inhaling. It still smelled like her.

****

Rana found Levin against a wall in the empty ballroom, lying on his stomach with his face buried in his shirt. He took occasional shaking breaths, as if he'd been crying for a while.

She left him alone and entered the hall but stopped walking before she returned to the other room. She closed her eyes and swallowed. *I should have stopped him.*

Since they'd left the church, she'd tried not to blame herself. Peter was the one who'd kidnapped Maggie and pulled the trigger. But if Rana had kept Levin at the hotel, Peter wouldn't have known about Maggie. She would still be alive.

Her brain said it wasn't her fault, but her gut told her the opposite. Unable to reconcile the two, she exhaled and entered the group's ballroom. Her half-brothers and a few others sat on the floor in a circle, talking about Levin. Dante scooted over to make room for her.

"Did you find him?" Daniel asked.

"Yeah." Her voice cracked. "I missed him the first time I checked in there."

Jeremy wrung his hands. "Are you okay?"

She nodded. "I just . . . I can't imagine how much he hurts." She wiped her tears with her open hands. "He's over there sobbing into the shirt Maggie gave him. That black one he wore today."

"Oh. I didn't know she gave him that." Daniel leaned back onto his elbows.

"Yeah. Two nights ago. He snuck out to see her." She stared at the floor in the middle of the circle. "Before we left the camp, my mom asked me to watch him. I told her I would." She squeezed her eyes shut, as if that would stop the tears. "He told me he was meeting her at the park last night. I tried to talk him out of it, but I didn't stop him from leaving."

Dante placed his hand on her shoulder. "Why did she tell you to watch him?"

She wiped her tears again and met his eyes. "She was afraid he'd do something foolish because he wanted to see Maggie so badly."

He squeezed her shoulder. "You can't blame yourself for this."

She wished she could agree.

****

"Levin, wake up. Dinner's here." Rana shook his arm.

He lifted his head off the shirt and remembered where he was. "I don't feel like eating." He laid his head back down.

"I can bring you something if you want. We can eat together, just the two of us. You don't have to talk if you don't want to."

When he didn't reply, she left and returned five minutes later. He sensed her closeness and smelled Chinese food, and his stomach growled. Sitting up, he put his shirt on, and she handed him a plate.

Rana twirled noodles around her fork. "Dr. Craig says we're leaving tomorrow morning."

"Where are we going?" He held the conversation for his sister, but even talking hurt. He took a bite of one of his favorite foods–an eggroll–and his stomach turned.

"San Diego. All of Uriah's people are there now."

"I don't think I can do this anymore, Rana." It was the only conclusion he'd reached in his hours of solitude. Why should he keep doing this? He'd already lost his love, his future, his only reason for staying with the group in the first place.

Well, almost his only reason. The other reason interrupted his thought with her words.

"I know. I can't imagine what you must feel. But Dr. Craig thinks we could beat the whole lot of them there. And then this will all be over."

Over? Levin scowled. How could any of this ever be over? Nothing would be like it was.

He shook his head. "You don't need me there. None of today would have happened if it weren't for me."

Rana sighed. "That's not true–"

"If I hadn't snuck out last night to be with her, she would still be alive. They wouldn't have been able to find her." He strained his jaw. "I've only been thinking of myself this whole time. You guys would do better without me screwing everything up."

"Levin, we need you." She connected with his eyes. "I need you."

He stared at his food, unable to eat it. Rana picked at her sesame chicken.

Leaning forward, he focused on her until she looked up. "You're smart. You'll figure it out."

She gestured with her fork. "That's not the point! This is everyone's fight. You can't just quit."

Heat rushed through his body, and his heart pounded. He clenched his fist. *Of course I can quit!* He jumped to his feet and held out a shaking hand. "He killed her, Rana." Pressing his lips together, he swallowed. "He shot her in the head with me three feet away." Adrenaline bubbled to the surface, cranking up his volume. "I was right there, and I didn't do a damn thing! So what makes you think I can do anything in San Diego? Huh?"

Shock filled his sister's eyes.

He took a long breath. "It's not you." Pain fired up in his jaw from clenching it so hard. "I'm sorry."

He rushed out of the room, leaving Rana alone with both of their dinners.

****

She screamed his name, and he ran through the dark, towards her. Why was her voice getting softer?

"Maggie!" he yelled.

Her voice became a muffled cry. His legs wouldn't move quickly enough.

Bang!

Levin jolted awake; his heart pounded. He took deep breaths and remembered where he was–his apartment.

A banging sound came from the door. He rolled onto his side and hoped it would stop, but it continued, followed by voices saying they were worried about him.

The girl's voice was Rana's.

He rose from his bed, still wearing his clothes from yesterday, and went to the living room to answer the door. Rana stood alone on his porch, her hair wet from the falling drizzle.

"Who were you talking to?" he asked.

"Dr. Craig. We've been waiting for ten minutes. He wanted me to leave, but I need to make sure you're okay."

"Dammit, Rana. Why can't you just–" His eyes went to her shirt, and his shock stole his words for a moment. "Where did you get that?" It was black with white writing–identical to the one Maggie gave him and that he still wore.

She stared at him and said nothing. He looked past her when he sensed movement.

The members of his group emerged from around corners and behind the vans to fill in the space behind her. They all wore black shirts with white writing.

I DIDN'T COME HERE TO LOSE.

He blinked several times as he surveyed the sea of black. Even Dr. Craig wore the shirt.

Levin glanced at the ground and cleared his throat before focusing on Rana. "What are you doing?"

She took his hand in hers. "We need you. You're part of us, no matter what."

Daniel and a few others voiced their agreement from behind her. Jeremy stood with his hand on the back of his neck and tears in his eyes.

Rana continued, "Let us help you get through this. Maggie wanted you to be home with her. You wanted that, too. Well . . . we all want to go home, and we need you to get us there. Come with us."

His half-brothers and friends echoed what she said.

"We need you."

"Come with us."

"Do it for Maggie."

Levin held his breath, unable to take it all in. He gave up on saying anything else and hugged his sister.

Chapter Twelve

Levin shoved some clothes into a gym bag and zipped it shut. Leaving it on the bed, he stared at it, then surveyed his room.

He'd been in such a stupor yesterday he'd barely comprehended being here. Home. With his own sheets on his own bed and his own clothes in his own closet.

Clothes that Maggie had touched and a bed she'd shared with him.

An ache took hold in his gut as an image of her waking next to him the first time flashed in his mind, the memory he'd dwelled on when he prepared to propose to her. She was supposed to wake up next to him every morning for the rest of their lives. Instead, she'd never wake up again.

He looked down at his shirt, at the white writing. This was the last shirt of his she'd touched.

A wave of nausea hit him.

This shirt was different. It was special. And his sister had somehow bought forty-something clones of it to convince him to do something he didn't want to do.

Darting from his room, he rushed out to the parking lot, where Rana and the others waited for him. By then, the slow drizzle had given way to a steady, cold rainfall.

Rana left one of the vans and met him on the sidewalk. "Where's your stuff?" She held her hand over her eyes, shielding them from the drops.

"I'm not coming." He crossed his arms, not caring about the water running out of his hair and down his face. "I can't. Okay? You guys shouldn't expect . . ." His voice caught. He turned his head to the side and cleared his throat. "You shouldn't have done that." He pointed to her shirt.

She glanced down at the white letters. "We wanted to show you we care."

"This . . ." He put his hands on his hips and turned away from her. "This was something we had. Together. You shouldn't have come here." He tilted his head towards the van. "Go back to the others."

Before she answered, he rushed inside, slamming the door behind him. He paced back and forth, but his energy didn't drop. With a yell, he punched a hole in the wall.

****

Rana gazed out the van window, watching Levin's apartment building shrink as they traveled away from it. She wanted to climb into a hole and bury herself; she'd been so certain her plan would work. The matching shirts were supposed to show Levin they all stood with him, and that Maggie brought them all together. It was a way for Maggie to be with them.

Instead, he'd stormed away from her. They had to leave him alone, wounded to his core.

Her eyes pooled with tears, and she leaned her elbow against the window's base. Resting her chin in her hand, she stared even more intently at the passing scenery, crying as silently as she could.

"Wanna talk about it?" Destiny asked.

Rana wiped her face with her open hand. "I don't know. I . . . I can't believe we're leaving him behind."

"We don't have a choice." Destiny put a hand on Rana's shoulder. "This is a huge loss for him. He's probably still trying to make sense of it."

"How can anyone make sense of it?" She sniffed. "He shouldn't be alone. If anyone finds him here, he'll have to . . ." She choked on the words.

Destiny leaned towards her. "Fight by himself?"

Rana nodded.

"Well . . ." Destiny sighed. "We'll have to hope no one finds him. None of us can even guess what he's going through. He needs time to heal."

Rana leaned back in her seat. "I wish he'd let us help him do that."

****

Levin woke on his bed a few hours after Rana left. He rubbed his unbandaged hand, still sore from punching the wall.

What the hell was Rana thinking? She wouldn't do something like that to intentionally hurt him. She knew he couldn't possibly hurt more.

Didn't she?

He sat up, and a dizzy spell caught him. Nausea settled in his stomach along with something else: hunger. He hadn't eaten since yesterday morning, and it was already the middle of the afternoon.

Trudging to the kitchen, he tried to think of what he could manage to choke down for the sake of survival. He didn't want to eat anything; in fact, wasting away seemed like a reasonable option.

The kitchen had little to offer: cans of soup among seasonings and a box of croutons. The fridge was empty. He'd sent Walt over to clean it out after they'd arrived at the camp, not wanting to return to rancid perishables.

He held a can of soup and grimaced at it, then put it back. Maybe a sandwich from his favorite restaurant would be more appetizing. But first, he needed a shower, if for no other reason than to get out of the shirt that had Peter's and Maggie's blood on it.

He undressed on the way to his room, leaving his clothes on the floor as he walked and not caring they were there. His normally fastidious nature gave way to his grief.

Upon reaching the bathroom, he set the shower to hot and glanced at the mirror, shocked at what he saw.

He left the water running and walked to the mirror, staring at his reflection. His eyes were puffy, his hair was greasy, and a dark beard had started to grow in. Drops of blood had dried on his neck.

He put a hand on either side of the sink and leaned towards the now-steamy glass. He wiped his hand across it.

In spite of all the ways he had thought about what happened in the church, he hadn't realized until now that this face–his face–was the last thing Maggie saw. He squinted at himself.

What did she see when Peter pointed the gun towards him? Fear? Determination? Hope that he would save them both? He squeezed his eyes closed, hoping that in the short second it took for Peter to turn the gun back to her, she couldn't understand he'd failed her.

Taking a long breath, he opened his eyes and reached up to touch his cheek. His hand was bandaged, and it hurt. He focused on it, then back on the mirror. It had steamed up again.

Finally stumbling to the shower, he adjusted the temperature and stepped inside, but images of Maggie flooded his mind. He leaned against the wall with his head down, mindlessly letting the water flow over him.

****

Several hours after leaving Denver, Rana and the group stopped at a laundromat in Grand Junction. The smell of some of her peers–those who hadn't packed enough clothes–had become intolerable, even with regular showers.

A few of her friends washed the black shirts, but Rana wished she could take them away. Not only had her plan failed, she had over forty reminders surrounding her.

As she loaded the washer, a man cleared his throat from behind her. She turned.

"Do you have a minute?" Dr. Craig held his phone up and wiggled it.

Rana nodded. "Let me finish this real quick." When she started the machine and turned around, he was gone. She walked to the front of the laundromat and found him standing outside.

He looked up from his phone when she met him. "I've been tracking the news in Denver. There's a story about what happened at the church." He held the phone out to her.

Why did he want her to read it? She reluctantly took the phone and held her breath.

The body of a young woman who apparently died of a gunshot wound was found with an unconscious man in an abandoned church yesterday. The man, who police believe was the shooter, was badly beaten, sustaining multiple facial fractures. He has been in a coma since police found him and is now hospitalized in serious condition. There is no word on who might have beaten him. Authorities are not releasing his identity at this time. Police have not been able to identify the woman and are requesting the public's assistance. She is described as Caucasian, 5 feet, 5 inches tall with shoulder-length light brown hair, brown eyes, and appears to be in her early twenties. If you think you may know this woman, or if you can offer any tips on who assaulted the man, please contact the Denver police.

Rana exhaled and handed the phone back to Dr. Craig, relieved they hadn't connected Levin to the beating. "We should tell them who Maggie is."

"I agree. But right now I'm more worried about Levin."

Rana's mouth went dry. "Why?"

"He stayed in Denver, and he has an injured hand. If Peter wakes up and talks, or the police are able to connect Levin to the beating, they'll easily find him. He'll likely be charged with assault and fleeing the scene, at least."

Rana glared into his eyes. "Fleeing the scene was your decision."

"I'm aware of that." He pocketed his phone. "We need to get Levin out of Denver, and quickly."

Rana shifted on her feet. This information would have been helpful four hours ago. "How?"

"I've spoken with Eric. He's agreed to take you back in one of the vans. I was thinking your half-brothers should go, too. We'll meet up with you in San Diego."

They were going to get him. Hope filled Rana for the first time since the shirt idea hadn't worked. While the news report wasn't an ideal reason for Levin to rejoin the group, it was a reason. And for his safety, it had to work.

****

The sun had set by the time Levin made it out of the apartment. He stood in line at his favorite sandwich place, hoping its familiarity would offer some comfort. Instead, it reminded him of all the things that would now feel different in Maggie's absence. She'd only come here with him twice, but it was enough for him to sense the void. He even remembered what she'd ordered–turkey with cheese and lettuce. Hold the tomatoes.

Swallowing the lump in his throat, he moved up in the line, and his eyes went to a TV mounted on a wall near the door. Tuned to a local news station, it flashed a familiar scene. Levin stood as still as possible, as if moving would allow strangers to see his pounding heart and the heat rushing to his face.

A female reporter stood on the street in front of the old church. Aside from the news crew's light reflecting off the broken glass in the nearest windows, the building was cloaked in darkness.

An image of Maggie's body in the basement flashed through his mind, as vivid as reality. He could smell the sweat and the blood, hear the gunshot, and feel the crunching bone. A thin layer of sweat covered his forehead.

He clenched his free hand and forced himself to focus on the TV.

"Thanks, Bill," the reporter said. "I'm here at the abandoned St. Michael's church downtown, where the body of a young woman who apparently died of a gunshot wound was discovered yesterday. She was with a man police believe is the shooter. He was badly beaten…"

Levin stared at the screen, transfixed. This story was about him, and though he had trouble comprehending all of the reporter's words, he gathered that the police didn't know who Maggie was, and they were looking for whoever beat Peter.

He glanced at his injured hand, evidence of his role in yesterday's nightmare. He'd haphazardly redone the bandage after his shower. Daniel's bandage had at least appeared professional.

"Can I help you?"

Levin looked back to the counter. The line had disappeared, and he stood five feet from the register.

He quickly weighed his options: he could leave, drawing attention to himself and his hand, or he could pretend like nothing was wrong and get something to eat in the process.

Trying to bury his nerves as he approached the counter, he mentally planned the route he'd take out of Denver as soon as his to-go order was filled.

****

Rana climbed into the van that would leave as soon as her brothers were on board. Though she'd been tired when they arrived at the laundromat, she didn't think she'd be able to sleep until Levin was back with them.

Isaiah plopped into a seat in the back. "So, what's the plan?"

"We go to his apartment and tell him the truth." Rana picked at a rough spot on her thumbnail. "He'll have to come with us. Denver is the worst place for him to be."

"What about identifying Maggie?" Daniel asked.

She sighed. Leaving Maggie unidentified seemed deplorable, but getting Levin back was their first priority. "We'll figure that out after we get him. We don't need to risk getting on anyone's radar before we're all together."

Jeremy twisted around in the seat in front of her. "Have you told him we're coming?"

She shook her head. "I've been texting him, but he hasn't responded. I don't think he's going anywhere."

****

Levin made a quick stop at his apartment to grab some clothes and used the little cash he had to fill the car's tank, hoping it would be enough for him to catch up to the others. If it wasn't, he'd be stuck wherever he ran out of gas. Using a credit card would make it too easy for authorities to track him.

After an hour on the road, he reached into his pocket for his phone and found an empty pocket.

He'd left his phone on the night stand, charging. It had been there all day.

He swore and did a U-turn.

After forty minutes, he found himself turning right at an intersection where he should have gone straight. Straight would take him to his apartment. Right would take him to Maggie's.

He couldn't remember deciding to go to her place. Something drew him there. Maybe it was knowing he'd never go there again, wouldn't hold her in that place again. He wouldn't even walk through the door.

The news report had said Maggie hadn't been identified yet. Levin planned to call her parents with a story about how he couldn't reach her, hoping they'd make the connection, but not until he'd left Denver.

No one had any reason to be at Maggie's apartment. He could risk one last visit.

He drove slowly in front of her building. Her porch light was on, but the inside of the apartment was dark. Stopping by the sidewalk, Levin surveyed the grounds: a few people walked to other apartments, but they didn't seem to notice him.

He left the car running and walked to her door.

****

Rana cupped her hands around her face and peered through Levin's front window. His apartment was dark. She turned towards the parking lot: his car wasn't there.

She returned to the van. "He's not here."

"We noticed." Daniel looked out the side window, towards Levin's front door. "What do you want to do?"

Rana slumped in her seat. "He's not answering his phone either. Let's wait for a bit. Maybe he'll come back."

But what if he didn't? They didn't have another plan, and they had no way to reach him.

Would they have to head to San Diego without him again? Rana squirmed at the thought.

****

Levin held up his hand to knock–his broken hand. He stared at it.

Why was he here? Maggie wasn't. As much as he wanted to pretend he would knock and she would answer, standing across the threshold and beaming, that would never happen again.

He pounded the door frame with the side of his fist, leaving it there. He closed his eyes as the ache in his gut grew.

"Hey, is that your car?" a woman asked from behind him.

He turned. "Yeah." His voice cracked.

"You need to move it. You're in the fire lane."

Levin placed his fingers on Maggie's door. "Sure. I was just leaving."

****

After another failed attempt to reach Levin, Rana shoved her phone into her pocket. They'd been waiting for an hour, and he still hadn't returned. Staying here much longer could be risky, if the cops figured out Levin's connection to the church. Her half-brothers filled the time with their own theories.

"If he went out for food, wouldn't he be back by now?"

"Maybe he didn't go out for food. Maybe he went to a movie or something."

"N…no. He w…w…wouldn't do that."

"Why not? Maybe he'd want an escape."

"Levin didn't go to a lot of movies when things were normal." Rana kept her eyes on his apartment. "He wanted to be alone. That's why he shut us out."

"So, where is he?" Daniel asked.

Silence filled the van for a minute.

"Maybe he went to the police," Jeremy said.

Rana's heart raced. "Why would he do that?"

"We had to leave Maggie with Peter at the church yesterday. Maybe he said something to direct the police there. If he hasn't seen the news, he might not know the cops are looking for him, too."

"Or," Daniel shifted in his seat, "they already found him."

Her throat tightened. She accessed a news site on her phone. There weren't any new reports about Maggie. If Levin had just gone there, though, or if he'd been arrested, it would be too soon for updates.

"Where's the police station? Let's drive by and see if his car is there," Daniel said.

"What if it is?" Rana asked.

Daniel shrugged. "We'll have to leave him there."

Rana's stomach sank. She focused on the entrance to the complex, begging Levin's car to appear.

****

Levin turned onto the main road heading to his apartment, stopping at a red light at the next intersection. The police station was within sight.

He crouched in the seat a bit and dropped his bandaged hand from the steering wheel, as if his very presence would draw attention. He sat up straighter when a familiar van pulled into the station's lot and parked in the back.

That couldn't be right. His group was headed to San Diego. They were probably near Vegas by now. Squinting, he leaned towards the windshield, searching for features that would place the van with his group.

The car behind him honked. Levin drove through the intersection, eyeing the van as he passed. The turn into the parking lot was just ahead.

It can't be them. Why would they be here?

He was halfway past the entrance when he decided he had to know for sure. Turning sharply, he entered the lot on the wrong side. Thankfully, no cars were trying to leave.

Parking next to the van, he peered through the passenger window. Eric sat in the driver's seat.

Levin slumped. Why was Eric here, and at the police station, of all places?

The van's door opened and Rana jumped out, running for him. Levin stepped out of his car, eyeing the building.

She wrapped her arms around him. "The cops are after you."

"I know." He pulled back. "So we shouldn't be here."

A uniformed officer left the building and walked towards them. Levin's pulse skyrocketed.

The officer turned, heading for a cruiser parked one row over.

Levin let out the breath he was holding. "Let's get the hell out of here."

****

As they waited for Levin to grab his phone from his apartment, Rana drummed her fingers on her leg. What if stopping at the station had alerted the authorities to their presence? No one had tracked them yet, but driving to the cops' front door might have done the trick.

She winced at the foolishness. They couldn't get out of the city quickly enough. Ironic, considering Denver was where Rana planned to end up when this was over.

Levin climbed in and sat in the seat in front of her. Holding a first aid kit, Daniel moved next to him. "Can I fix that?" He pointed to Levin's bandage.

"Yeah. I did what I could." Holding out his hand, he let Daniel undo the messy job.

Rana leaned forward, watching Daniel work. "That means you got a shower, right?" She knew he had. She smelled the difference immediately.

He nodded.

Maybe that meant he felt a little better. Enough to care about personal hygiene, at least.

Levin pulled his phone from his pocket and turned it around in his hand.

She watched for a few seconds. "What are you doing?"

"The cops don't know who Maggie is."

Daniel stopped bandaging Levin's hand, holding the gauze in place above his wrist. "And you're thinking of calling them yourself? From a phone registered to you, the guy who put Peter in a coma?" He raised his eyebrows and resumed his work. "That might not be smart."

"No, not the cops. Her parents. I can say I haven't been able to reach her." He looked out the window and sniffed. "They'll have to make the connection on their own."

Rana scooted forward and touched his arm. "It's better than them finding out much later, don't you think?"

Daniel secured the bandage, and Levin turned backwards in his seat. "I know what happened to her, and . . ." His voice caught. "It would be better for them to hear the truth from someone who loved her."

"But you can't do that." Rana focused on her brother's eyes. "If you tell them the truth, you expose your role in what happened. And you'll expose the rest of the group. I know lying about this sucks, but it's the only way you can say anything."

He cleared his throat. "Yeah. You're right."

Rana and Daniel watched him as he told Maggie's mother about not being able to reach her, how weird that was, and how worried he was. He kept the call short. By the end, his voice shook. He wasn't doing a good job of hiding his grief.

Chapter Thirteen

As the van neared Las Vegas early the next morning, Levin's phone vibrated in his pocket. He frowned at the unfamiliar number. Who would call so early?

"Hello?"

"Levin? This is Doug Shaw, Maggie's father."

"Oh. Hi." He shifted in his seat. "Did you find her?" He squeezed his eyes closed.

"Yes, we did." The line was quiet. Levin imagined her dad fighting back tears. "Levin, I hate to tell you this, but . . ." He cleared his throat. "She was . . . she's dead."

"What?" Levin winced. He was no actor. The sound of his voice could communicate emotions he wasn't supposed to have in this lie. "What happened?"

The van pulled into a gas station, next to one of the other vans, and his half-brothers piled out.

"She was shot. The police found her in an old church downtown. We have no idea why she was there."

Levin gripped the phone tighter.

Rana put her hand on his shoulder as she stood, looking into his eyes. He nodded to assure her he was okay–anything to get her out of the van. Something about lying to this man made him want to run to solitude.

Maggie's father cleared his throat again. "They think she might have been kidnapped. They're still trying to sort everything out."

Levin put his elbow on his knee and leaned his forehead against his bandaged hand, sharply pulling back when the pain registered.

His sister finally joined the other PRs gathering between the vehicles. Levin stayed firmly planted in his seat, watching them and listening to the father of the woman he'd loved so dearly.

"Maggie loved you, Levin. She talked about you all the time."

I loved her too. He didn't say it, fearing it would betray the shock he was trying to fake.

He stared at his lap, struggling to force words from his mouth. "I, um . . . I don't know what to do with this."

"I know. Where are you working now? California?" His question came from the false information Maggie had given him.

"Yeah."

"Okay. As soon as the police release her body, we'll plan a service for her. I'll let you know."

"All right. Thanks for letting me know." He ended the call, took a breath, and focused out the window while he wiggled the tips of his bandaged fingers.

Across the parking lot, Dr. Craig stood with all three drivers. He had a serious expression and talked with his hands. Eric put one hand on his hip and the other over his mouth. The other drivers had their arms crossed; one staring at Dr. Craig and the other at the ground.

Whatever Dr. Craig was telling them didn't look good.

****

With all the PRs reunited, Rana claimed a seat in the back of the van with Destiny and Amaya. She would have preferred to sit with Levin, but Daniel asked her to let him have a turn. She'd tried to analyze Levin's emotional state since they picked him up from Denver, but the silence, staring, and sleeping were hard to gauge. He'd always been a private person. He was likely keeping the effects of what happened to Maggie bottled up tight when he was around so many other people.

"Will your brother be okay?" Destiny asked, pulling Rana's attention away from the back of her brother's head.

Rana turned sideways, leaning back against the window. "I hope so. I've seen someone get pretty messed up after something like this before." She tried to keep the worry from coming through in her voice.

In the seat in front of Rana, Amaya turned around and sat on her knees. "What do you mean?"

"My step-dad was in the army. He saw his friend die in combat, and he had a hard time adjusting to normal life after that." Rana sat forward and looked out the window. "I worry that Levin will have problems like that." She had watched Walt internalize his experience, resulting in a wreck of a human being. She shuddered to think Levin might end up like that.

"Oh. That's hard to say. We don't know exactly what he saw," Amaya said.

"Dr. Craig told me some of what happened, so I wouldn't be shocked if Levin told me." Rana curled her legs up, hugging them. "It sounded pretty bad. I'm not sure how I would react if I saw something like that happen to someone I love." She stared out the window to keep her imagination in check, but it didn't work. "Ugh. Let's talk about something else. How did you learn to throw spears, Amaya?"

"Javelins. I competed in the decathlon in high school. Thought that part would transfer to this. I've been trying to teach Travis." Her face twisted. "He's sort of getting it. Did you know Levin shot a bull's-eye while we were practicing at the camp?"

Rana scrunched her eyebrows. "Really? The shots I saw weren't that impressive. They looked like little arrow flowers sticking out of the ground."

Amaya laughed. "Well, I guess he won't do much shooting with his hand all bandaged up."

They were back to that conversation. Rana turned to Destiny. "Weren't you in Dante's group?"

"Yeah. Our dad taught me how to shoot, but I never took lessons like Dante did. I learned how to play the cello instead."

"You should have brought it. You could lull the bad guys to sleep."

Amaya laughed again. "You're funny!"

Rana grinned as Daniel moved to sit next to Amaya. "How's it going back here?"

"Good." Amaya turned and leaned against the window. "Did you get bored up there?"

"Levin wanted to sleep, and things are always more interesting when you're around."

Giggling, Amaya brought her hand to her mouth. Daniel inched closer to her.

Rana tilted her head, staring at them.

Destiny smacked her on the arm, drawing her attention. With raised eyebrows, she nodded rapidly.

"How long has this been going on?" Rana clapped her hand over her mouth. That came out louder than she'd intended.

Daniel and Amaya twisted around. Daniel's cheeks were a little red. He glanced at Amaya before focusing on Rana. "Since a week before we left the camp."

"How did I miss that?" Rana replayed her interactions with both of them since then and came up empty.

Amaya laughed. "You were pretty distracted with wanting to go home, my friend. And . . ." She pursed her lips. "We were keeping it quiet. For Travis."

"Why would your brother care?"

"Our dad's always been strict about us dating." She waved her hand. "I don't need Travis shooting his mouth off the first chance he gets just because."

"That makes me feel better. I guess." Rana glared at Daniel.

He held his hands up in surrender. "Hey, don't look at me. I wanted to shout it from the roof of my cabin."

Laughing, Amaya shoved his shoulder, and they both faced forward.

Rana shook her head. "Does Levin know?"

Neither of them answered.

Seeing a new relationship would be tough for Levin to see, but she supposed it was bound to happen–all these teenagers grouped together would pair off eventually. Her mind went to Jason. Where was he? She'd barely seen him since the day they left the camp. Perhaps he was avoiding her. She wouldn't have blamed him.

Tucking one ankle under her leg, Destiny turned towards Rana. "Can I ask you a question?"

She nodded.

"Are you upset? About the shirts? I noticed you look away when you see someone wearing theirs."

The sinking feeling in Rana's stomach returned. After washing her shirt, she'd stuffed it into the bottom of her bag, where she wouldn't have to see it. Her friends seemed to enjoy wearing theirs, though. "Kinda." She picked at her fingernail. "I was so sure it would work. That they'd convince Levin to come with us."

"I think they made an impact. That's something, right?"

"I guess." She focused on her friend. "I figured we didn't have anything to lose. It's like . . . Maggie bringing us all together, you know?" She caught her breath as she felt herself starting to cry. "I'm pretty sure he thinks I took something special he had with her."

After a pause, Destiny asked, "Did you ever meet her?"

"Yeah. Around the time we learned about the Project. She was amazing. Levin really loved her." She wiped her cheeks with the back of her hand.

Destiny put her hand on Rana's shoulder. "You guys are close, huh?"

She nodded. "I can't imagine doing this without him."

****

Levin woke as the vans parked in front of an elementary school. The lot contained only one car, odd for a . . . what day was it? He'd stopped keeping track since his birthday.

When the van stopped, Dr. Craig faced everyone behind him. "The wife of one of my guys is the principal here. She's allowing us to use her gym and fields today. I'm hoping you'll have time to warm up and practice before we have to go anywhere. Collect your things and head inside."

Everyone crowded into the gym. A colorful, cartoonish tiger was painted on the bricks that composed one wall. Levin sat on the floor under the tiger's head and leaned against the bricks. The others seemed content to fill the middle of the floor.

When he finished talking to a woman–Levin assumed she was the principal–Dr. Craig walked to one side of the gym. He clasped his hands in front of him. "Before I begin, I want you to know it's been a privilege to work with all of you. You know I raised Scott as my son. Since his death, it's been comforting for me to take on a type of father role. And for that, I want to thank you."

Levin sat up straighter. Where was this going? It had an air of finality that his other morning announcements lacked.

Sighing, Dr. Craig scanned the group. "I say all that to say this: no matter what happens today, you will all be going home tomorrow. This morning, I was informed the money from the Project that I've been funneling into a secret account has stopped. That means Uriah's people either noticed my account and shut it down, or the government department supporting us audited them and cut off their funding. We believe the latter possibility is the correct one. In any case, we can no longer support you. The mothers and children still at the camp are flying home today."

That didn't make sense. What about the money in the trust?

Muttering took over the room, and Dr. Craig raised his voice. "This makes today's mission all the more important." The crowd quieted. "It is quite literally our last chance. It's now or never. If we win– and I'm sure we will–you can all go home in safety, knowing that Scott's faction will fall apart after another fallen leader and no money to support their operation."

"Does that mean the Project is dead?" Jeremy asked.

"In a manner of speaking, yes, the organization that was Project Renovatio is dead. Though the original Project died when Scott led the split in its ranks. The only way to re-establish our research and to continue paying your mothers their yearly allowances is for me to appeal to the heads of the department that was funding us. That could take years and would probably end in failure if the funding ended because of an audit."

Levin studied his siblings and friends, who desperately wanted to get home. To live freely. What Dr. Craig had told them hinged on them winning, but . . .

"What if we lose?"

Dr. Craig stared in Levin's direction. "If we lose, Uriah will likely continue operations with money from his supporters and the families he recruits. It will be harder for him because the Project mothers won't be getting their money anymore, but it won't be impossible. It will look much like a cult. We can't say for sure, but once you are all home, we think his group would start by trying to recruit you–however they need to do it." He paused. "That's why we can't lose."

Levin tried to reconcile the dissonance racing through his brain. He'd already lost everything, yet here he was among his peers, all hoping for a brighter future. Now that he was away from Denver, Levin didn't care if he ever went home. Everything about that place reminded him of Maggie.

"Uriah's holding a gathering this evening," Dr. Craig continued, "in the auditorium of a high school across town. Our plan is to arrive hours before he does and wait. The auditorium is dark and has catwalks. You should all wear your black shirts. We'll hide on the catwalks until Uriah starts speaking. When I enter the auditorium to confront him, that is your cue. Surround the audience in a horseshoe shape. I want the archers to stand in the back. Uriah will probably get angry and threaten me.

Those of you with weapons can raise them at that point. After that," he sighed, "I don't know what will happen. You'll have to trust your instincts."

"Wait." Levin stood. "You want us to fight *over* the audience? Around them? How does that keep them out of danger?"

Dr. Craig stepped into the crowd, towards Levin. "Consider who we're fighting. This is . . . like a pep talk. A motivational gathering to get more people to willingly join them. We don't believe the PRs they've gathered so far will be there. We will have Uriah and whoever is with him outnumbered. The question will be if they try to fight us anyway, or if those in the audience see *us* as the threat." He walked the rest of the way through the group, stopping feet from Levin. "We don't think that will happen. The audience won't be armed. But we have to do whatever it takes to stop Uriah. I think you understand that more than anyone."

Levin's throat tightened. Fighting misled bystanders wasn't the reason he was here.

"So," Dr. Craig held out his hands and turned back to the others, "use this morning to practice. Archers, Amaya, and Travis: there's a large field outside. Gather whatever you can for target practice. I saw a recycling bin when we entered the building. Start with what's in there. Everyone else, use whatever space you find appropriate. I'll be around if you have questions."

He stepped towards the door, but a voice stopped him in his tracks. "We need a name. We can't be Project Renovatio if they are."

Dr. Craig nodded. "Okay. Does anyone have a suggestion?"

After a few seconds of silence, Dante stood. "I was talking about this with Travis earlier and did a little research." The crowd quieted. "'Renovatio' means 'renewal' in Latin. I thought we could use another Latin name. How about Project Liberatio? It means 'deliverance.'"

The chatter that followed indicated a general acceptance of Dante's suggestion.

"Excellent." Dr. Craig nodded. "Project Liberatio. I can't wait to watch it succeed."

Chapter Fourteen

Rana sat with Brent against the gym wall as they watched the Taekwondo group practice. Wincing when Levin threw kicks and occasionally a clumsy punch with his uninjured hand, she focused on Brent and brought up the first non-combat subject that came to mind. "Did you know about Daniel and Amaya?"

"Yeah. I th...think he figured I www...wouldn't have the p...p...patience to tell anyone." He smiled.

She laughed. "I just found out this morning. How long have you known?"

"About a week."

"A week? Wow."

She watched Levin practice hands-free Taekwondo for a few minutes before saying, "He looks goofy."

"Who? Levin?"

"Yeah. I think we should tie his hands behind his back and complete the image." Scowling, she tilted her head, as if that would improve the display before her.

Brent laughed. "He c…can't shoot with the b…b…bandage. This is p…probably his only choice."

"Hmmm." Rana centered all her attention on Levin.

They watched in silence for twenty minutes before the group took a break, and Jason jogged over to them.

"Haven't talked to you for a while. You doing okay?" He stood over her with his hands on his hips and tried to catch his breath.

"Okay enough. Just trying to help Levin get through all this, you know?" She suppressed a wince. What would her excuse have been had nothing happened to Maggie and Levin had nothing to get through?

"Yeah. It's tough." He glanced at the empty space where he'd been practicing. "I think he'd better figure out a way not to fight anyone directly tonight."

"Why?" Rana sat up straighter.

"Weren't you watching? He can't do much without using his hands. He needs to be able to block, at least."

Rana considered Jason's words. "I guess he can make the group look bigger by just being there."

"Maybe. I gotta go get a drink." Jason left them and entered the hallway.

Rana stood and approached Levin, who leaned against the wall under the tiger. "Jason's worried you won't be able to defend yourself tonight."

He held up his right hand. "Because of this?"

"Yeah. He said you can't even block."

"I'll be all right. I can duck and kick. And I have my other hand."

"You weren't using that one either–at least not for strikes."

"It's bruised. I figured if I'm gonna hurt it more, I'd wait 'til tonight. Don't worry, I'll be fine."

"Levin," she sat down next to him, "why don't you stay with the first aid group? You can still make us look bigger that way. And you won't have to worry about anyone hitting either hand."

He glared at her. "This is what I came here for. I'm not bailing out now, especially since you went all the way back to Denver to get me." He raised his eyebrows. "Okay?"

She grimaced. "Okay." She jumped to her feet and returned to Brent but didn't sit down. "I'm going outside. I don't think I can watch him anymore."

Brent nodded, and Rana left the gym.

She walked outside to a large field. The archers had set up several boxes and plastic bottles to use as targets. While weaving his arrowhead between his fingers, Dante paced behind the archers and smiled at Rana when he saw her approach. Amaya and Travis practiced with the spears on the far end of the field. Daniel sat on the grass behind everyone and watched.

Rana plopped on the grass next to him. "How's it going out here?"

"It's impressive. Most of the archers can shoot bottles right off the top of the boxes. Amaya's getting the bottles too. Travis–not so much."

Rana laughed. "I can't believe I didn't know about you and Amaya."

"You've been a little distracted. And we weren't exactly advertising it. She still thinks Travis doesn't know."

"He knows?"

"Yeah, we share a cabin. He knows."

"You share a cabin with Levin too, and he didn't know."

"Levin's been lost in his own little world. First he could only think about getting to Maggie, and now . . ." He sighed.

Rana watched Amaya throw a spear. "What's gonna happen after today? I mean, Dr. Craig said everyone's going home. Where's she from?"

Daniel looked down and pulled blades of grass. "Missouri. And I don't know what's gonna happen. We haven't been seeing each other that long. I'm thinking of moving to Denver, if I get into the medical school there, that is. She's in school for medical engineering." He watched her throw before continuing. "I really like her. I guess we'll just have to figure it out." He faced Rana. "How's it going inside?"

Rana rolled her eyes. "Levin looks ridiculous. How's he supposed to fight with a broken hand?"

"It'll be tricky." Daniel pursed his lips. "He didn't break his left hand, so he at least has that." He scrunched his eyebrows. "If he takes a direct hit to the broken one, he'll be in bad shape."

"What do you mean?"

"It would be so painful that he wouldn't be able to function. I think he would collapse."

147

She inhaled. "Can we keep him out of it?"

"I don't see how. This is why he's still here."

Daniel echoing Levin's words irritated her. They were both right, though. Levin was here to fight. It's why they were all here. And his being here, where an injured fighter could become a dead one, was her doing. Maybe she should have let him stay in Denver.

They watched arrows and spears sail towards the targets for a few minutes.

"Do you think we'll ever meet our father?" Rana asked, partly to keep any conversation going and partly to keep from worrying about her brother.

"Our Greek father? I doubt it. I think the point of the Project picking fathers from all over the world was so they couldn't be found. How would that work? He'd show up here and go 'So, how many kids do I actually have?'"

She laughed. "Let's see: you, me, Levin, Jeremy, Eliot, Brent, and Isaiah. Oh, and Scott, I guess." She paused. "Am I the only girl?"

"Huh. I've never thought about it, but I guess so. Dayla and Janie have different fathers."

Rana watched the archers for a few minutes before she decided she wanted an answer. No other groups of half-siblings had only one girl. Why was theirs different? "I'm going back inside. I'll see you later."

In the hall, Dr. Craig paced around a small area and held his phone like he didn't know what to do with it.

She approached him. "What's going on?"

He looked up. "I just found another article from the Denver newspaper about Maggie. They've identified her, so that's good." He shook his head. "It also says Peter is awake, but he can't talk. If he gives them Levin's name, Levin could have real problems."

"Like what?" Rana was running out of ways to worry about her brother.

"Hard to say. He may be charged with assault. On the other hand, Peter might not say anything because Levin watched him shoot Maggie."

Standing in place, she faced Dr. Craig without looking at him.

"Do you need something, dear?" Dr. Craig asked.

She shook off the previous conversation. "Oh, yeah. I want to ask you something, and if we're going home tomorrow, I might not have another chance."

"Okay. What is it?"

"Why am I the only girl from the Greek father?"

"Oh, figured that out, did ya?" He gestured to a bench. "Let's sit down."

They sat, and Dr. Craig started his explanation. "When the Greek father signed on with Project Renovatio, he had one stipulation: that only one girl be created from his cells. He wanted to know there was one special girl out there somewhere. I think he imagined she–you–would be unique. He knew the boys would obviously benefit from the higher endurance and strength and perhaps blend with other boys. But the girl–by design, she would be stronger, smarter, and set apart."

She blinked several times as she tried to absorb the meaning of his response. "Do you think he'll try to find me?"

"I don't think so. I think he just liked the idea of you. Look . . ." He sat up and turned towards her.

"All PRs were designed to survive a global disaster. But from how the Greek father described his request for only one girl–which was unique to him, by the way–I sensed he hoped you'd do more than simply survive. He wanted you to be a leader. So he made sure you'd be special from the start."

Mouth agape, she stared at the floor. What was all that supposed to mean?

Dr. Craig patted her on the back and stood. "I can talk to you about this later if you want." He gestured with his phone. "I have to talk to Levin now, though." He left her alone on the bench.

What had her Project father had in mind for her? The only father she'd known was Walt, and he'd been checked out from the family for most of the last five years. She couldn't imagine she'd been created for some defined purpose.

****

After reading the article, Levin handed the phone back to Dr. Craig. "Do you think Peter will talk?"

"I don't know. If he does, and the police reach you, describe what happened on the most basic level without bringing the Project into it. Say Peter had a personal grudge with you and kidnapped Maggie to get to you. You beat him in the rage that resulted from watching him shoot Maggie. They might not even charge you with anything." He put his hand on Levin's shoulder. "But he might not say anything. You're the only eyewitness to what happened. He might want to keep you out of it."

Levin leaned against the wall and slid down to a crouching position. Everything Dr. Craig told him to say was technically true. He put his hand over his mouth and stared straight ahead before looking up at Dr. Craig. "How did the cops end up at the church? How did they find Maggie?"

"After we were back at the hotel, I had Eric make an anonymous call about hearing a gunshot coming from the church."

"And you weren't worried that Peter would report me?" Levin stood, meeting Dr. Craig's eyes.

"I didn't see that I had a choice. The alternative was to leave Maggie there until someone happened to discover the scene, and that might have been days or weeks. Would that have been acceptable to you?"

Levin clenched his jaw.

"And besides, I thought you killed Peter."

Levin's stomach turned. "I'm not a murderer."

Dr. Craig put his hands on Levin's shoulders and looked him in the eyes. "I know you're not."

Levin pulled away and rushed out of the gym. He quickly found the bathroom and secured himself inside a stall, leaning against a wall and trying to catch his breath.

What would have happened if Dr. Craig hadn't entered the church basement when he did? Would he have continued to beat Peter until he was dead? Was he capable of that?

He leaned his forehead against the door and closed his eyes as rage built in his gut. He squeezed a tight fist with his unbandaged hand and took slow breaths in and out. His heart pounded, and beads of sweat formed on his face.

Yelling, he punched the door, sending a shock wave up his arm.

When he emerged, he found Jeremy standing by the sinks, waiting for him. "Are you okay?"

Levin shook his head. "I don't know."

Chapter Fifteen

Everyone changed into their black shirts and boarded the vans for the hour-long ride to the high school. Levin was last to board his van. Those inside were eerily quiet; most stared out windows or straight ahead without speaking. Dante bowed his head and mouthed inaudible words.

Levin found an empty seat next to Jeremy and across the aisle from Dante. His thoughts alternated between what might happen when they got to the school and what might happen if Peter gave the police his name. On one hand, he and his peers could take down a dangerous leader and allow for them and dozens like them to live in safety. On the other, he could end up in jail.

Fifteen minutes after leaving the elementary school, Dante expressed a long sigh while running his fingers along the edges of his arrowhead.

"Are you okay?" Levin whispered.

He looked up. "Oh. Yes. I was just praying. I thought we could use all the help we can get."

"Are you scared?"

"No. I believe we're ready." He studied Levin. "Can I ask you a question?"

"I guess."

"What are you fighting for?"

Levin scrunched his eyebrows. "What do you mean?"

The others started their own conversations, and Dante raised his voice above a whisper. "I assume you left the camp planning to fight for Maggie. I was just wondering what's driving you now. Is it revenge?"

Levin thought for a moment before responding. "No, I don't think that's it. I wasn't even gonna leave Denver. When Rana and the guys came back for me . . . they did it so the cops wouldn't track me down. So I didn't really have a choice."

"You have a choice about whether or not to fight."

Did he have a choice? "I can't sit back and watch while the rest of you fight."

"Sure you can." Dante turned, facing Levin. "You were injured in Denver. No one would blame you if you sat this one out. You'll still be there to make the group look bigger. That may be all we need."

The knot in Levin's gut remained. He drummed his fingers on his leg. "No. I can't do that. We all want to get home, right?"

Dante tilted his head forward. "Do you?"

After a long moment, Levin shook his head. "I'm not sure."

"Can I tell you what I think?"

Levin nodded.

"I think you're here for your sister, your half-brothers, and your new Project friends. They want to go home and get back to their lives in safety, and you can help them do that. You lost your reason for going home, but not your reason for fighting with us. It would be understandable if you were here for revenge. But I don't see that in you. I think your purpose here is greater than that." With his arrowhead, he pointed around the van. "I think we are the reason you're here."

As Dante's words hung in the air, certainty covered Levin, so strong it crowded out the grief that had made its home in his spirit. When he looked at those around him, his friends and family, his reason for being here, a smile tugged at the corner of his mouth.

****

Rana and Destiny reclaimed their places in the back of the van. Levin and Dante started talking, and Rana tried to listen to what they were saying, but other conversations drowned them out.

"You're being really quiet," Destiny said.

Rana faced her. "Oh. Yeah. I'm just thinking."

"Is it about today?"

"No. Dr. Craig told me something, and I'm trying to figure out what to do with it."

"What did he tell you?"

Rana turned towards Destiny. "I figured out I'm the only girl with the Greek PR father. Turns out, he only wanted one girl created from his cells. This somehow makes me special. Or something." She squinted.

Destiny laughed. "That's cool! Your father knows there's one girl out there somewhere he can claim as his, and she's you. It means he had a purpose in mind for you. It does make you special."

"Ha. No pressure though. What would he say to the fact that I was just an average high school student before all this Project stuff? Probably not the Superdaughter he had in mind."

"Really?" Jason popped up from the seat in front of them and turned around. "There's nothing 'average' about you at all. Never has been. I'm sure if you ever met your Project father, he would be proud of you."

Rana scowled at him. "Who said you could listen?"

"A simple 'thank you' would suffice." He winked at her.

She smirked. "So what do I do with it?" Flattery wasn't close to the real answer she'd been hoping for.

"Nothing specific." Destiny shrugged. "You were made to be different. Use that to do something important."

Rana nodded and looked out the window. "I like that."

The vans pulled up to the side of a large high school. The visible part of the building was two stories high with a brick exterior and no windows. It had to be the auditorium.

Dr. Craig moved from van to van. When he left one, the Project kids exited the vehicle, retrieved their supplies, and followed a stranger wearing Dockers and a burgundy polo shirt into the building.

He reached her van last. "Uriah and his people aren't here yet. We're not expecting them for two hours. We wanted to give ourselves plenty of time to get in our places without the risk of being discovered. You'll be waiting and doing nothing until then, so I hope you have a song stuck in your head."

A few PRs chuckled.

He pointed out the window. "Gather what you need from the back and follow that man. He'll show you where to go."

Dr. Craig left the van and entered the building by himself. Everyone else unloaded, retrieved their things, and met the man waiting on the sidewalk. Rana made a point of connecting with Levin before they went inside.

"How are you doing?" she asked.

"Better." He looked at her, and she gasped. The despair that had draped him was gone.

"I'll say. What happened?"

"Dante just has a way of explaining things really well."

She smiled. "Yeah, Destiny does that too. They're kinda becoming our personal gurus, huh?"

He grinned, and she suppressed the urge to cry. "It's good to see you smile again."

He put his arm around her shoulders and squeezed.

The man led them through the double doors. They entered a lobby that displayed posters from past musicals, and Rana's pulse quickened. This was a place for art, not for a potentially deadly battle, if that's what it came to.

We're just here for appearances. We won't have to fight anyone.

She wished her gut feeling agreed.

They walked through another set of double doors and into an auditorium lit by dim, evenly spaced lights on the side walls. A stage adorned with thick, maroon curtains rested at the base of several inclined rows. It matched the auditorium at her own school almost exactly–she could almost smell the remnants of the smoke bombs the seniors lit onstage as a prank last year.

They walked into a wide aisle in the middle of the room, with rows of seats above and below where they stood. The man turned to face them.

"My name is Derek. I'm one of Dr. Craig's inside guys. I've been working among Uriah's group since he took leadership. I'm here to help you get situated for tonight, but I can't stay long, so please listen carefully. Above us is a network of catwalks." He pointed above him. Rana could barely see the black shine of the metal. A few sets of eyeballs peered down at them; the rest of their group was already up there.

"You're going to wait there. Your black shirts will help you hide in the darkness. We don't think anyone will notice you. You can talk quietly until you see me come back, and then you must be silent. I'll be returning with Uriah's people to prepare for tonight, and I'll take the lead of the operations in here to limit outside attention. I'll make sure they only operate stage lights and keep the room dark. Your job is to sit and wait until Dr. Craig enters the auditorium and gets Uriah's attention. You'll enter from the back, through the lighting booth. File down the sides of the seats and surround the crowd. I believe Dr. Craig told you the rest."

Jeremy raised his hand. "Can I ask a question?"

"Yes, but quickly."

"Who will be in the crowd?"

"The front row will be Project kids and families Uriah turned to his cause. The rest are new families that Uriah led here. They'll be hearing the bulk of his message for the first time. That's why we want you to have your weapons, though we don't expect you'll need to use them. You outnumber those working for Uriah, so it would be foolish for them to engage you. We want the families to see you as an opposing force, one that will free them instead of control them. A few of them are here as the result of . . . violent persuasion."

Rana took a long breath.

"Follow me to the lighting booth, and I'll show you how to access the catwalks. Don't go far out into the auditorium: the closer you are to the stage, the more likely you'll be discovered. Stay as close to the lighting booth as you can."

They followed Derek through the booth. He directed them to climb up a short ladder, and Rana found herself on the black metal. Her peers split between the catwalks on either side of the auditorium and the perpendicular piece that connected them, allowing the group to sit in a horseshoe shape.

Dante and three other archers walked farther into the auditorium, arming their bows towards the seats and talking. He leaned on the rail and aimed, then shook his head and said something before they joined the others in the back of the room.

Rana reached Dante at the same moment the lights went out. She held her hand in front of her face, amazed by the complete darkness. Squinting, she leaned towards his outline. "What were you guys talking about?"

She jumped a bit when he answered; he was closer to her than she thought. His breath met her cheek. "We thought we could stay up here to shoot."

"It won't work?"

"We can technically do it, but if there are people in the seats, we could hit them. I don't want to risk it. Dr. Craig needs us to make the group look bigger, so we'll line the back, like he said." His hand found her shoulder. "Come on, let's sit with the others."

Rana grasped the cool rail as she shimmied down the catwalk. Worried she might step on someone in the darkness, she bent over as she moved in an attempt to identify those she passed. She stopped when she reached Brent.

"I'll find Levin," Dante said. He put his hands on her shoulders and scooted past her.

Rana sat next to Brent and placed her first aid kit behind her back.

"Are you nnn…nervous?" Brent asked.

She leaned towards him. "A little. Should all of us in the first aid group gather in the same place, away from everyone else?" It would be foolish for her group to be in the middle of the conflict, especially if any actual fighting occurred. Her peers needed to know where to get help.

"It's a good idea. Hhh…how about in the back r…row?"

"That should work. I'll go tell everyone."

Rana crouched as she walked around the group, paused when she recognized the first-aid members, and told them the plan. She rejoined Brent when she finished. "Now, we tell everyone else." She turned to Isaiah, who sat on her other side. "If you're injured, meet the first aid group in the back row of the seats. Pass it down."

Isaiah nodded and repeated the message to the person sitting on the other side of him. She leaned over Brent and told the person sitting on his other side. She hoped her message made it all around to everyone intact. Memories of her elementary school classes playing Telephone flashed in her mind. Some of those messages weren't even close to the original one.

"I guess now all we have to do is wait," she said. Talking to Dante and forming the first aid message had provided a welcome respite from the sense of dread that insisted on covering her, but now all she had to do was worry. She tried to balance her fear with Destiny's words.

Maybe you'll do something important.

Chapter Sixteen

Levin sat between Dante and Jeremy on the catwalk and occasionally talked in whispers, but most of the group waited in silence. He tapped his fingers on the dusty rail in an effort to relieve his anxiety. The complete darkness was a trap; a quick escape would be impossible.

After what felt like half a day, the doors to the auditorium opened, and light spilled in from the lobby. Derek loudly cleared his throat as he entered, perhaps as a signal for his group to be quiet. Other men followed him. One was tall, blond, and dressed in a dark suit, contrasting with Derek's business casual attire.

The men stopped at a sound booth behind the lower section of seats. Levin couldn't hear what Derek said, but it appeared he was explaining something to the blond man. Derek fitted the man with a wireless microphone that rested around one of his ears.

The blond man had to be Uriah.

Levin held his breath. After a few heart-stopping minutes, during which Uriah scanned the space, Uriah and the other men left the auditorium. Derek climbed the steps through the upper section of seats and entered the lighting booth. He turned on the stage lights and crawled under the control panel.

Why did he do that?

Before long, people entered the auditorium, dropped their phones into a canvas bag held by a man dressed like Derek, and sat in the seats of the lower level. Some looked content; others appeared tired and stressed. Derek stood by the sound booth and talked to a professionally-dressed woman while pointing at the house lights and shaking his head. The woman followed Derek into the lighting booth, where she worked dials and sliders on the control panel, scowling when her actions apparently didn't produce the desired result.

Derek had disabled the lights when he crawled under the panel. Levin silently laughed to himself.

Uriah's visitors almost fully occupied the lower level of seats, and chatter filled the space. Why were these people here? There wasn't much evidence of violent persuasion, but why did they give up their phones so easily?

The tall, blond man took the stage by himself. "Good evening. I'm so happy to see you've all joined us tonight. My name is Uriah."

They chose to be here?

Uriah paced the stage and gestured with his hands, like a motivational speaker. "Some of you received letters. Others allowed my supporters to visit you in your homes. For whatever reason, you're here because we believe the same thing: we are in a position to make the world a better place.

"But before I get to that, let me tell you about myself. I am not a Project Renovatio child, but I am the older brother of two of them. My family was one of the first Scott approached with his unique idea of using genetically gifted individuals–you–to control society. PRs could establish themselves in a place of superiority, running the government as they saw fit, and everyone would benefit as a result."

Levin had to get a better look. This guy was indirectly–or maybe directly–responsible for Maggie's murder. Creeping down the catwalk towards the stage, Levin clenched his fist. The anger in his gut intensified with every step.

"I want to carry Scott's vision a bit further. There are problems in the world that are seemingly impossible to solve. Famine. War. Pandemics. Now, remember why you were created. Your very bodies were made to survive such circumstances. I ask you this: what if you used your gifts to not just alleviate these problems, but solve them? Is that the kind of world in which you want to live?"

A few in the crowd yelled their approval while others clapped.

Someone touched Levin's leg. He twisted around. Jeremy was crouched behind him, gesturing for him to return to the others. Levin waved him away. No one could see him up here. He tightly gripped the rail with his unbandaged hand.

"Some of you are gifted with superior language skills; you may become diplomats and end wars. Some have great endurance to harvest resources and the intelligence to know how to efficiently use them. You may find the cure for cancer. My friends," he held out his arms, "the dreams of world peace and all of humanity living long, healthy lives are finally within our grasp. I ask you: what can *you* do to make the world a better place? How can *you* use the gifts you have to not only better the lives of your fellow men, but to ensure a lasting legacy for yourselves?"

Many in the audience clapped, and Levin understood how Uriah managed to be so persuasive. He was all about feeding the human ego. He must have convinced those working for him that torture and murder were necessary for the greater good.

As Uriah took a breath, Dr. Craig's voice permeated the room. "And what will *you* do when you find yourself working for a power-hungry organization with no option to leave, for doing so would risk your own well-being and that of your family?"

Uriah held a hand over his eyes, shielding them from the spotlight, as he peered into the darkness. "Who is that?"

Walking down an aisle adjacent to the upper section, the old man emerged from the shadows. "My name is Dr. Steven Craig."

"Oh, Dr. Steven Craig! The man who refused to stand behind his own son in his mission of benevolence." Uriah held his arm towards Dr. Craig and shook his head.

"Scott was severely misguided in his mission, and it would only lead to pain and death." Dr. Craig moved forward and stopped between the upper and lower sections of seats. "Project Renovatio was designed as a stopgap for humanity, a way for people to survive and rebuild, not to rule and oppress."

Levin stood over the crowd as more movement filled the auditorium: his peers were walking down the side aisle and surrounding the spectators, as Dr. Craig had instructed them to do.

Crap. He'd missed entering with the group, and now he'd have to join them by himself, separated and exposed. He silently cursed at himself for not reclaiming his place between Dante and Jeremy in time.

He creeped into the lighting booth and made his way to the side aisle.

"I suggest to you a new option," Dr. Craig said, "that we call Project Liberatio."

Rather than walk behind and past Dr. Craig, Levin moved along the back row, forcing the first aid group to let him by. Rana glared at him, as if asking where the hell he had been.

Uriah chuckled. "Please. You can't just make your own group and give it a fancy Latin name. Project Renovatio is the true way, and we will usher in a new age of safety, security, and health–"

"Liberatio means deliverance." Dr. Craig raised his voice. "Deliverance from force, from violence, and from the deception you are offering. There are many smart, strong, diplomatic people in the world with no ties to Project Renovatio, and they haven't been able to solve the problems you mentioned. What makes you think a few hundred genetically gifted individuals will be able to solve them?"

Levin found a spot in the back corner, between Isaiah and Jeremy. He exhaled. Uriah didn't seem to have many people here; he counted five standing around the space. His group could easily take them out. Contrary to Levin's unspoken fear, none of Uriah's workers carried a visible firearm.

While Levin assessed the situation, Dr. Craig's voice echoed through the room. "When you fail at achieving your lofty goals, what are you left with? I submit," he directed his attention to the audience, "that what Uriah is offering is not prosperity for everyone. Scott believed PRs would rule–they would be superior by design and oppress or even torture any who disagreed as a way to secure wealth and power. Once the ideals he describes fail," he pointed to the stage, "that is where you'll find yourselves: as either the oppressors or the oppressed."

"You're wrong!" Uriah yelled. "Scott knew the gifts possessed by PRs were being squelched. You," he directed his attention to Dr. Craig's group, "were made to be so much more!"

Levin's stomach turned at hearing the same words Peter used seconds before he shot Maggie.

"I can't help but notice your little uniform you have there." Uriah pointed to Dr. Craig. "But I believe one of you did lose." He surveyed the group. "You lost someone very special. Didn't you?"

Levin stood quietly, suppressing his urge to rush the stage. Uriah obviously didn't know which one he was, and exposing that fact wouldn't help anyone.

Uriah shook his head. "And now you hide among your foolish brethren. It's no wonder you didn't save her."

Levin clenched his uninjured hand. It took every muscle to stay in place. Jeremy grabbed the back of his arm and whispered, "Don't take the bait. That's what he wants."

"That's enough," Dr. Craig said. "Why don't you tell the people here how your right-hand man murdered an innocent young lady in front of the man who loved her? Or how your people injure and torture the families of PRs who don't share your vision?" Dr. Craig scanned the crowd. "But you don't need to tell some of these people about that, because they already know, first hand. Is that the vision of benevolence you're preaching?"

Uriah sneered. "She wasn't innocent. She was holding him back from his full potential. He couldn't see it, so we had to make him see it."

"And what will you do to others who get in the way of the potential of PRs? Kill them too?" Dr. Craig yelled.

Levin sensed movement in his peripheral vision. A group of young adults was surrounding them. Some held clubs and the rest held switchblades. Levin faced the young man–a boy, really–standing behind him and holding a club.

"I hope you realize you weren't the only ones to bring an army with you tonight." Uriah chuckled, and his group of young people positioned themselves for attack.

The boy behind Levin raised the club above his head and lunged. Levin deflected the attack with his forearm. Planting his foot against the boy's chest, Levin kicked him away.

The boy recovered and rushed Levin again, this time with more force. Levin caught the club in his good hand. The boy pushed him between the rows of seats until he fell. Levin landed on his injured hand. It curled under him in spite of the immobilizing bandage.

Levin squeezed his eyes closed and shook in place as he tried to absorb the throbbing in his hand. He struggled to breathe. *Get up! You can't lose!*

He positioned his other hand under himself and lifted, but a dizzy spell took hold. His hand slipped and he fell onto his elbow. His muscles shook more violently as his body absorbed the blow.

No one else tried to attack him. He could likely stay safely hidden between the rows.

****

Rana couldn't decide where to focus after Uriah's group crowded around hers. Pairs of fighters moved into the center aisle and into the rows of seats, shoving the audience towards the center of the room. Dante and a few other archers used arrows to stab; the proximity of the other group ruled out the possibility of shooting.

A minute later, injured members of Dr. Craig's group ran to the upper section of seats. Destiny cradled her bleeding arm and approached Rana.

"Let me see." Rana sat Destiny in a seat and tried to sound calm as the shouting around them bounced off the stone walls. Destiny uncovered her arm, revealing a deep cut. Rana wouldn't be able to suture anything here, so she retrieved some gauze and wrapped the arm. The bandage became blood-soaked almost immediately.

Rana looked at the others in the first aid group. Everyone was dressing wounds. If the battle continued much longer, they would be overwhelmed.

She turned her attention to Levin's position, but he wasn't there. She scanned the auditorium as panic took hold. Where was he?

Leaving her post, she ran towards the place she last saw her brother. A blinding pain on her head took hold the same moment a club-holding guy appeared next to her. She collapsed and brought her hand to her head, blinking until the flashes of light before her dissipated. Swallowing, she forced herself to stand. She had to find Levin.

She yelled when her feet left the ground.

****

Shouts filled the space surrounding Levin; some belonged to his peers. A nearby yell sounded like Rana, but that didn't make sense. She was stationed in the back with the first aid providers.

He shook off the thought. His group needed him. Staying hidden wasn't an option. Stopping Uriah depended on them winning this battle, and Levin needed to help them do that.

He opened his eyes, took a labored breath, grabbed the seat nearest him with his good hand, and struggled to his feet. He kept his injured hand behind his back in an effort to protect it from another blow. When a club-bearing girl appeared in front of him, he hesitated.

He hadn't considered hitting a girl. She looked Rana's age and had black hair. She would look just like Rana, if he squinted.

She lunged towards him, and he deflected her attack without performing a counter strike.

Taking two steps back, she scowled. "What, you afraid?" She attacked, and the club landed on his left shoulder.

He groaned in pain and kicked her away. She slammed into the wall before reorienting herself and facing Levin again.

She seemed to wait for him to attack. "You afraid to hit a girl?"

Raising her club, she ran at him. He reached up and grabbed it, yelling when the pain in his shoulder fully registered in his brain. He yanked the club away.

They both froze in place when Uriah's voice boomed over the loudspeakers. "Stop!"

Levin glanced at the stage and gasped. Uriah held Rana by her hair.

He ignored the throbbing in his hand and removed the bandage.

****

Do something! Anything!

Rana's scalp burned as Uriah yanked on her hair. Holding her breath, she twisted to elbow him in the ribs but changed her mind when he pulled again. She squeezed her eyes closed as the gun barrel pressed into her temple.

"Why won't you understand?" Uriah's fury laced his words. "We want to do something great, and you're in the way! Don't you realize you leave us no choice?"

"You have a choice. We all have a choice. And no one is choosing to be controlled by a faction with grandiose visions," Dr. Craig yelled from somewhere in the crowd. Rana couldn't see anything beyond the blinding spotlights.

"I'm trying to make you see the truth, even if this is what it takes!" Uriah pulled Rana's hair, sending pain from the club strike down her spine.

"She's a PR, Uriah! You don't hurt PRs!"

"We've come too far for that silly notion anymore. A PR who is against us is more of a threat than an average person who is against us. All the more reason to remove them, don't you think?"

****

Levin grabbed Isaiah's bow, took an arrow from the quiver at Isaiah's side, and climbed onto the seat behind him, positioning himself above the crowd. He groaned through the agony in his hand and shoulder as he loaded the bow and fired.

****

The pressure on Rana's head released. A scream came from the audience. She opened her eyes. Uriah was reaching for an arrow protruding from his neck. Mouth agape, he gasped for air. His blood spurted and soaked his sleeve and the collar of his suit coat.

Rana knocked the gun from his hand and kicked him in the chest, and he fell to the ground. She ran away from him and out the door her abductor had used to carry her to the stage.

She returned to a different scene in the auditorium. The archers stood in the second row of the upper section of seats with their bows armed. They aimed at the members of Uriah's group, who were clustered in the aisle separating the upper and lower sections. Dante stood in the middle of the line in spite of the blood running down the side of his face from a cut on his forehead.

The few unconscious members of Uriah's group lay on the floor surrounding the seats. Dr. Craig and Derek led the people in the audience out of the auditorium.

Rana approached Daniel. "What on earth happened in the last thirty seconds?"

"I'm not sure." Daniel spoke through a wad of gauze he held on his nose. "After Levin shot Uriah, the archers all moved and armed their bows. Everyone else pushed Uriah's guys here, to the middle." Daniel seemed to remember why Rana didn't know what happened and asked, "Are you okay?"

She moved her hand to the place the club had struck her; it still throbbed, but she didn't want to think about it. "Yeah. Did you say Levin shot Uriah?"

Daniel nodded. "He ran outside after it happened."

Rana studied the injured members of her group.

"It's okay. We got this. Go." Daniel gestured to the door with a head tilt.

Rana ran outside. The crowd stood together on the grass as Dr. Craig started telling about Scott and the original mission of Project Renovatio. Some of them cried.

She found Levin sitting on the curb by himself. He held his right hand in his left and had closed his eyes. She sat next to him.

He opened his eyes, leaned over, and wrapped his arms around her.

Chapter Seventeen

"You were designed to be unique, to survive. Perhaps you can solve some of the world's problems, but do it in your own lives. Start in your own towns."

Levin listened to Dr. Craig's words as he sat on the curb and held his sister. Was everything they had gone through the past four months really over? They would be home tomorrow.

Rana pulled back. "Daniel told me what you did."

He took a breath and managed some words through his shaky voice. "He was going to kill you like Peter killed Maggie." A chill ran through him. He suppressed the shudder. "Are you okay?"

She nodded. "I was so scared. I couldn't see you out there. I couldn't see anybody." She put her hand on her head. "He pulled on my hair so hard." Smiling, she said in a shaky voice, "But you got him, right?"

He smiled back. "Yeah. I got him." The split second it took for the arrow to leave his bow and plant itself in Uriah's neck flashed in his mind. He cringed.

"But how? You didn't bring a bow with you."

"I borrowed Isaiah's." He looked at his throbbing hand. The swelling had increased dramatically in the last ten minutes. It started to resemble a baseball glove.

"You hurt it again, huh?"

"I couldn't shoot with that bandage on." He faced her. "But I don't care about my hand. You're okay. That's what matters."

She took his injured hand in hers. "I'm just glad you didn't miss."

He focused on her eyes. "I knew I wouldn't miss."

****

After the crowd dispersed, Levin and Rana joined Dr. Craig on the grass. Dr. Craig looked away from the building, held his wrist to his mouth, and said, "Scene is clear" into it.

Rana studied the watch on Dr. Craig's wrist as they approached from behind him. "Were you talking to someone?"

He twisted around. "Oh, no. Just talking to myself."

She tried to get a better look at the watch. It appeared normal, but what he said wasn't something people say to themselves.

Before she could ask Dr. Craig to elaborate, Levin gestured to the departing group. "You're letting them go?"

"We don't have a choice. They had only started to warm up to Uriah's ideas. I think I countered his message enough that they won't consider going back to it."

"Go back to it? Didn't you say the faction would fall apart without Uriah?" Rana asked.

He nodded. "That's likely. But we can't control what any of them do with their own resources."

Rana stood in place and scowled. Would she and her friends have to fight another leader like this? She shuddered at the thought.

Levin stepped towards the door. "What about the ones inside? Why didn't Derek tell us about them?"

"He didn't know." Dr. Craig caught up with Levin. "I think Uriah figured out that Derek was working for me. I'm going to deal with Uriah's group now."

The three re-entered the auditorium to the same scene Rana had left, except someone had turned on the house lights. Dante hadn't tried to wipe the blood from his face. Jeremy and a few others had collected the weapons from Uriah's group and loaded them into one of the bags that had held the audience's phones.

All of Uriah's group members–about forty of them–sat on the floor in the center aisle. Rana's peers treated their injuries while Brent and another girl in the first aid group carried the unconscious ones to the center. Uriah's body was still on the stage.

Rana sat next to Destiny in the last row. Levin sat with Daniel, whose nose had stopped bleeding, though it looked swollen. Dr. Craig stepped in front of the seated crowd, and the archers lowered their weapons.

"We don't want to hurt you." He clasped his hands in front of him. "I don't believe you wanted anything besides what Uriah preached on the surface. You want to solve many of the world's major problems. And for that, I commend you." He scanned the many faces focusing on him. "Can I ask how many of you are Project Renovatio children?"

Nobody moved at first. After a few seconds, one hand went up. Then another. And another. Soon, all who had worked with Uriah and who were still conscious had their hands up. Rana assumed the unconscious ones would be raising their hands too, if they could.

"Okay." Dr. Craig nodded. "I recognized some of my former Project employees. Do any of you know where they went?"

A boy answered. "No. They just took off and left us here."

Dr. Craig pursed his lips. "I see."

Rana analyzed Uriah's group–they were just like hers. What would have happened if Scott hadn't approached Levin all those months ago? Would they be on Uriah's side now? The people before her were possibly siblings to those she saw every day. Perhaps their similarities explained how they all managed to avoid more serious injuries: while they fought to defend their respective groups, they didn't intend to seriously hurt each other.

"How many of you served under Scott?" Dr. Craig asked.

No one raised a hand this time.

"Wow," Rana said to herself. Uriah had assembled all of these people in just the last two months.

"Then I should tell you about him, as he started this whole movement. He was a PR, and I raised him as my son. My wife died two years ago, and Scott couldn't handle the grief. He developed a warped sense of superiority. Unfortunately, he was also very charming and manipulative. He lured PR workers to his cause with the promise of wealth and fame through the recruiting of PR families.

"Uriah's message was different. He suggested that you," he gestured to Uriah's group with open arms, "and you," he turned to his own group, "have the power to change the world in a huge way."

A younger teenage boy stood. "So why won't you let us?" With clenched fists, he stepped towards Dr. Craig.

Dante armed his bow, and the boy glared before sitting down.

Dr. Craig looked at the boy. "You were all created for the same purpose: to survive and renew society if circumstances make that necessary and to pass your genetic advantages to your children. You do have the ability to change the world, but not in the way Uriah suggested."

"Okay, so how?" a girl near the front asked.

"Use your intelligence to solve medical mysteries, study the law, or invent things that will benefit society. Use your strength to build and maintain machines and infrastructure. Use your language to write books and songs. You don't have to work under a man like Uriah to make a difference in the world. You already have the tools you need to do that."

A girl in Uriah's group raised her hand.

Dr. Craig focused on her. "Do you have a question?"

"Yes. When Uriah talked to me and my family, I wanted to go with him right away." She started crying. "But my dad didn't want me to go. I think they did something to him so they could take me without it being a kidnapping. Do you know if he's okay?"

"I can't say for sure. However, you bring me to my next point." He paced a few steps. "We have only enough money to fly you all home. Then, all this is over." He turned his attention to the girl. "You can see your dad tonight or early tomorrow."

Rana kept glancing at Dante as Dr. Craig spoke. Blood ran from the top of his forehead, down his face and neck, and soaked into his collar. Yet he stood in place, unfazed.

"We'll fly you all to a few major cities where your families can pick you up." Dr. Craig pulled a paper and pen from his pocket. "Tell me where you live."

Dr. Craig wrote the cities as Uriah's former followers recited them. As he did, Rana made her way to the row behind the archers.

"Dante," she whispered over his shoulder, "come to the back so I can take care of that cut. The others can stand guard here."

He kept his place for a moment, then looked at Isaiah, who nodded. Dante climbed over the seat behind him and walked ahead of Rana to the opposite side of the room, removing his arrowhead from his pocket on the way. He sat next to Destiny. Rana found her kit and sat at his other side.

Rana retrieved some wet wipes from her kit and wiped the blood from around the cut. "You need a few stitches, but I can't do them here. I'll just bandage it up for now."

"That's fine," he said with a shaking voice.

She cleaned the wound and applied several layers of gauze to it. "Is there a story that goes with that arrowhead? I see you with it a lot."

"Oh, yeah." He held it up. "My grandpa gave it to me when I started taking archery lessons. He told me it's to help me be brave."

"You have it all the time, though." She taped the gauze and smiled playfully at him. "Are you worried you'll be a cowering mess if you don't have it?"

He grinned. "No." He turned the arrowhead around in his hand. "I've carried it around so long, it feels weird not to have it, you know?" His eyes connected with hers. "I think you're really brave."

She looked down, putting her supplies back into her kit. "Oh. I dunno."

"No, I mean it. Considering what happened, and now you're taking care of others."

After she retrieved a wet wipe, she met his eyes again. "I've been watching you stand there for fifteen minutes with blood streaming down your face because you had a job to do." She started wiping the blood from his forehead.

"Okay, I guess we're both brave. How's that?"

She smiled. "That works."

As she cleaned the blood from his skin, she glanced at his eyes. They were glued to her.

Looking away, she kept wiping. "What are you staring at?"

He placed his hand on top of hers, stopping her from cleaning his face. Holding her hand against his cheek, he took a long breath and whispered, "Thank you."

For the first time, she didn't look away from his gaze. There was something different about it, something . . . intense. She was so caught up in it, the only words she could think of were, "You're welcome."

She returned her attention to her task, and as she finished, she made eye contact with him a few more times. Every time, his dark eyes were watching her. A gentle nervousness gathered in her stomach the longer he sat there. When she was done, with his arrowhead in hand, he rose to rejoin his group but glanced back to her as he reached them.

Destiny moved to the seat he vacated. "What was that?"

"I don't know." Rana stared in his direction.

Chapter Eighteen

After Eric returned with the empty van, the members of Uriah's group loaded into all three vans, and the drivers took them to the airport. Soon after they left, Derek and two strangers walked onto the stage, wrapped Uriah's body in a tarp, and removed it. One man stayed behind with a mop bucket and removed the blood.

Levin kept his eyes glued to the stage, trying to reconcile how in becoming a killer, he'd also become a hero.

After the others had funneled out of the auditorium, Levin joined them on the grass as they waited for the vans to return. The warm night air and nearly full moon combined with the street lights provided a gentle ambience. Rana and the rest of the first-aid group took the opportunity to suture their injured peers. Moving his left arm into different positions, Levin decided his shoulder was bruised, not fractured.

He watched Rana stitch a cut on Dante's forehead. She smiled and talked while she worked, like she hadn't almost been killed just over an hour ago. Her resilience amazed him.

With a small grin, Dr. Craig stood on one side of the crowd and called for attention. The chatter quickly dissipated.

"I couldn't be more proud of you all." His voice caught. "I'd be lying if I said I wasn't worried about how tonight would end. But I'm grateful Uriah's group looked so much like you. I think it explains why there weren't more serious injuries."

He scanned the faces before him and paced. "I told you earlier you would all be flying home. There's been a slight change of plans. Because we wanted to put Uriah's group on planes, we don't have enough money for your plane tickets. However, after the vans return, you'll all load into them, and the drivers will take you home. Or close to home. Some of you will have to call your families to pick you up from a major city, if you don't live in one. It will take several days to make the journey." He looked at Jeremy and Eliot. "Especially if you live in Miami. If you want to contact your families to send you the money to fly home, you can certainly do that."

After a few seconds of silence, Jeremy cleared his throat. "This is our last chance to be with this group. I don't think any of us mind taking another road trip together."

Several others nodded. Dr. Craig grinned. "Okay. Which van you take depends on where you live." He indicated which vans would take which routes. Levin made a mental note to board Eric's van, the one traveling through the center of the country with a stop in Denver.

Dr. Craig clasped his hands in front of him. "Once the drivers reach their final city, they're going to sell the vans and fly home themselves. After that," he paused for a long breath, "the Project is over."

Silence covered them again, and Destiny broke it this time. "Sir, I want to thank you for everything you've done for us. You watched over us like we're your own kids. You helped us prepare for tonight." She started crying. "And who knows what would have happened if you hadn't come for us that night in the basement of the office building."

Others voiced their agreement with Destiny's words, and a few clapped. Soon, with the exception of Levin, the whole group applauded Dr. Craig.

What would have happened if he hadn't come for them? Scott had trapped them all. Would they have fought their way out? Levin had tried, and Scott had stabbed him. That might have been enough to scare some of his peers into siding with Scott.

Levin shook his head. If Dr. Craig hadn't shown up that night, he and many others here might have been forced to participate in Scott's delusion, at least for a while. They wouldn't have gone to the camp, but they still would have been yanked away from their lives.

Whether Levin wanted to admit it or not, his ability to live a normal life ended that night. He was part of a group designed to be different. They might have been able to blend into society undetected before Scott concocted his plan, but now, with ideas of genetically gifted superiority undoubtedly planted into the minds of some of Uriah's PRs, it was only a matter of time before their existence was revealed to the public. Whether the public accepted them was not something Levin could predict, though the thought filled him with dread. Historically, society didn't have a great record of accepting those who were different.

Dr. Craig nodded as the applause dissipated. "Thank you, Destiny. I know I'll remember how well you all worked together. I hope you all do as well." He stood in place for a few silent seconds. "This next hour or so will be your last chance to say goodbye to the people who won't be on your van and to exchange numbers. Take advantage of it. I'll shut up now and let you get to it."

Everyone stood. Levin scanned the faces and tried to discern who wouldn't be in his van. As he chose a direction, Dr. Craig stopped him, put a pen in his good hand, and walked away. He stared at it. Why had Dr. Craig done that?

There could only be one reason. Levin was supposed to collect phone numbers.

The meeting with the lawyer back in Montana felt like it occurred in a different life. Dr. Craig had charged Levin with potentially becoming the group's guardian, regardless of the events of the last few days. If something happened to Dr. Craig and they all faced danger again, it would be up to Levin to get them all to safety.

While searching for something to write on, he put his hand in his pocket and pulled out Dayla's note.

He unfolded it enough so the two blank half-sheets that composed its back showed. He couldn't write, so he walked around to the others and had them write their numbers for him.

Levin studied the names and numbers, hoping he wouldn't need to use them, but also thinking of a safe place to keep them. Cell phone contacts could get wiped out. Computers crash. On this paper was likely the safest place, as long as he didn't lose it.

Once he got home, he'd figure out a place to keep it. For now, he folded it and returned it to his pocket.

****

Rana found Destiny in the crowd right away and hugged her. "I can't believe I won't see you every day anymore."

Destiny pulled back. "I have a feeling I'll see you again soon."

"What do you mean?" Rana tilted her head.

Smiling, Destiny hugged her again.

"That didn't answer my question."

Destiny laughed. Rana stepped away from her. "I'll talk to you later, okay?"

Destiny stood there, smiling.

Turning around, Rana found Brent, and she hugged him. "Thanks for all your help."

He released her. "Y…you would have been fine. You're a nnn…natural." He winked.

"I'm glad we were partners, and I'm glad to have you as my brother. Let's get back to emailing, okay?"

"Yeah, a ph…phone c…c…call might take 'til Christmas."

She smiled, and after another hug, she turned and bumped into Dante. He grabbed her wrist and pulled her away from the group.

What was he doing? They walked across the sidewalk, stopping near the corner on the opposite side of the auditorium doors. He faced her.

"So," he ran his hand over his hair, "I wish I had the guts to talk to you before now."

"Why?" She cocked her head.

He sighed. "I've been . . . noticing you, since that day you came to get us for lunch back at the camp. You, um . . ." He rested his hand on the back of his neck and glanced at the sky, as if searching for the right words. Lowering his hand, his eyes connected with hers. "You have a beautiful, giving soul, and everything about you is authentic. The more I watched you–the way you speak, the way you move, your smile," a grin took over his face, "the more I found myself thinking about you." He took another breath. "And now I can't get you out of my head."

She blushed and looked at the ground in a futile effort to hide her red cheeks.

"I'm not freaking you out, am I?" He leaned over a bit to meet her eyes.

"Oh, no. I just had no idea." She suddenly remembered how often Dante happened to be wherever she was–that day at the camp, on the vans, in the ballroom–she'd thought nothing of it at the time, but now his behavior was obvious. He'd made an effort to be near her as much as possible.

"Yeah, I know. I decided I wanted to know Levin more before I approached you, since you're his sister. I wanted to know he would approve, especially since we're all living in such close quarters. Or we were." He looked at the ground and grinned.

"You talked to him about this, didn't you?"

"Not yet." His dark eyes met hers and lingered there. "It seemed inappropriate after what happened to his girlfriend. But I'll talk to him before we leave tonight. After this," he put his hand on the bandage taped to his forehead, "I felt like we connected."

Rana smiled. "I felt it too."

"And now we have to go to different states!" He dropped his arms to his sides and expressed an exaggerated sigh.

She laughed. "We need to exchange numbers. My phone is in my bag on the van, but Dr. Craig has a pen. Let's go back."

They joined the group and discovered Levin had a pen. Rana wrote her number on Dante's wrist. He took the pen and wrote his number on the inside of her forearm.

"So you can't accidentally wash it off." He raised an eyebrow at her.

She giggled. "Thanks."

A girl tapped Dante on the shoulder and asked, "Can I borrow that pen?"

He gave it to her, and she wrote on someone else's arm. They'd started a trend.

Dante gazed into Rana's eyes. "I'd better go talk to Levin, or I won't have the chance."

"Okay."

He grasped her hand and gave it a gentle squeeze. "I hope you don't mind if I call you very soon."

The nervousness in her stomach made its way to her chest.

He released her hand and walked into the crowd. She stood in place for a few moments before realizing she needed to say goodbye to more friends. She should have held onto that pen.

"I told you I'd see you again," Destiny chimed in from behind her.

Rana faced her. "Yeah."

Chapter Nineteen

Levin boarded the van with the others who needed to trek through the center of the country. Dr. Craig rode with them for some reason. Levin decided he would ask him about it later. For now, instead of taking his usual seat right behind the driver, he sat next to Rana in the back.

She had her phone out and was entering numbers into her contact list, copying the numbers from her arm.

"So, which one of those is Dante's?"

She looked up. "He said he was going to talk to you."

"He did."

"And?"

"I think it's great. I'm not sure you could find a better guy."

She blushed.

He laughed. "I didn't know you liked him."

"I didn't either, until tonight. I dunno, I guess the way he stood there guarding everyone even though he was hurt, and the way he talks to me . . ." she shivered.

"I never expected a guy who was interested in you to ask for my permission to date you. It seemed really important to him, though. I didn't know what to say."

Her eyes widened. "What *did* you say?"

"I believe my exact words were, 'Uh, what?' followed by 'If this is what Rana wants, then go for it. She's a good judge of character.'"

She covered her face with both hands. "I can't stop smiling!"

"Then I think you've found a good one. I hope you guys can manage being in different states for a while."

"I think we'll be all right. We can get to know each other over the phone and internet first."

Levin hugged her. "I have a good feeling about this."

"Me, too."

Rana released him and went back to putting the numbers on her phone and assigning them custom ringtones.

Levin left her and made his way forward to sit in front of Daniel and Amaya. Travis sat across the aisle. Daniel and Amaya held hands.

"I guess your little secret is out." Levin dropped into his seat. Back at the camp, Daniel had told him about Amaya and laughed when he'd said she wanted to keep it from her brother.

"It wasn't a secret. I knew all along," Travis said.

Amaya hit his arm. "Yeah, you stinker. You let me go all this time thinking you were clueless."

191

Travis smirked. "I wanted to see how long you could go pretending like nothing was going on."

Chuckling, Levin turned around, trying not to think about the new relationships forming around him. An emptiness settled in his chest, and he closed his eyes.

Someone sat next to him, and he looked up. Daniel had moved next to him. "You doing okay?"

"I will be. I was just trying to figure out how to think about home without Maggie."

Daniel pursed his lips. "Sorry. It isn't nice for us to act all couple-y around you."

"No, it's not that. This is my deal." Levin pulled his phone from his pocket for the first time since retrieving it from his bag. He turned it on: two new voicemails. "I'm gonna check these real quick."

The first message was from his mom saying that she and Dayla were home and she hoped everyone was okay. The other was from Maggie's father.

> *Levin, it's Doug Shaw. The police have released Maggie's body, and we're planning a service for her for next Saturday. We're hoping you'll be able to make it into town. Call me at this number and I'll give you the rest of the information.*

Levin disconnected and sighed.

****

A couple of hours into their trip, Levin moved to the open seat next to Dr. Craig. "Hey. I was just wondering why you're on this van."

Dr. Craig lowered his book to his lap. "I'm going to Denver with you. If Peter talks, I thought I should be there."

"I don't know if you need to do that. I'm sure you want to get home too." Dr. Craig was currently traveling away from his San Diego residence.

"No, it's fine. I sold my house when everything started going to hell with Scott. I was living with my nephew until we left for the camp."

"Oh. Okay."

"And if you do get into legal trouble, I think my testimony will help you. I'd like to be close by for a while, just in case."

"Why? What would you say?"

Dr. Craig stared at Levin before answering. "I'd say that Peter was terrorizing you, that he forced you to watch him kill Maggie, and your actions in attacking him were visceral reactions to the trauma."

Levin considered Dr. Craig's words. "Why are you protecting me? Is it because of this?" He pulled Dayla's note from his pocket and held it up, displaying the names and numbers. He moved it to his wallet, next to the lawyer's card.

"Partly. I guess you remind me of Scott, or how Scott was when his mom was still alive. It's not just that you look like him. He was thoughtful, and he looked out for others, just like you do. I see how you and Rana are together. I wonder how he would have been with a sister." He put his hand on Levin's shoulder. "I hope you don't mind me projecting my fatherly instincts on you."

"It's okay. Thanks for helping me." He stood. "And I'm glad you pulled me off of Peter."

"So am I."

Levin started to leave, but paused. He leaned close to Dr. Craig's ear. "What about the money?"

Dr. Craig scowled. "What do you mean?"

"You told everyone it was gone. But what about . . ." Levin raised his eyebrows.

"We're . . ." Dr. Craig leaned closer. "Saving that."

"For what?"

"For later. Remember how I told you about another group possibly threatening you?"

Levin nodded.

"Well . . . just keep your eyes open."

Levin left Dr. Craig alone and returned to his seat. It seemed the possibility of another threat was more than a possibility–it was a probability.

He scanned the van's interior, focusing on the carefree faces. He was the only one besides Dr. Craig who knew about threats, money, or had any kind of a plan. Their safety was in his hands.

Chapter Twenty

The van arrived in Denver the next afternoon. The driver dropped off Levin, Rana, Jason, and Dr. Craig at a restaurant near the interstate.

With her phone pressed against her ear, Rana walked away from the group. "Hey, Mom. Guess where we are."

"Oh my gosh! Are you here?"

Rana laughed. "Yeah." She stepped out of earshot of the others as she told Liz their location. "I have to tell you something really important about Maggie before you get us so you don't bring it up to Levin."

"About Maggie? What is it?"

Rana closed her eyes. It was bad enough that Levin would return home to a whole new reality, but over time, he would have to bring everyone else into it, too. She'd offered to tell their mother for him, and it was harder to form the words than she'd expected. How would Levin do this however many times it would take to tell everyone who had known Levin and Maggie as a couple?

She took a long breath to settle her nerves and quickly said the sentence to get it over with. "Peter murdered her in front of Levin a couple of days after we left the camp."

"What?" Liz paused. "Was she the girl they found in the church? I saw something on the news about a 20-year-old woman."

"Yeah. That's her."

The line was quiet for several seconds.

"I wish I knew before." Liz's voice sounded shaky. "How's Levin doing?"

"He was really bad at first, but he's been getting better. You can talk to him about it, now that you know, but wait until it settles."

Liz cleared her throat. "Okay. I'll come for you shortly."

With a shaking hand, Rana returned her phone to her pocket and sighed.

Today was a new start for her. Next week she'd be back at school and back on track to graduate early, and she'd already been texting with Dante. They hadn't waited a whole day before talking to each other.

But in this moment, Rana couldn't focus on how her own life had improved in the last couple of days. What would Levin have to focus on? They'd neutralized the threat that kept them confined to the camp, and aside from his job, she wasn't sure how else Levin spent his time.

Hopefully, he had something purposeful to hold on to.

****

As Levin watched his mother's car approach, a lump formed in his throat. Not only was it time to start adjusting to life without Maggie, he had to face talking to people about it.

Liz exited the car and gave everyone a hug, including Dr. Craig. "Rana didn't tell me you were here!" She faced Jason. "And I bet you're happy to be home."

He smiled. "Yeah. I was hoping you could give me a ride, if you don't mind. I live close to you, and I want to surprise my family."

"Oh, sure. But you'll have to pile into the back seat."

Liz's eyes were red and puffy, like she'd been crying. Levin peered through the car window. "Where's Dayla?"

"I left her at the house with Walt. I thought you might want to talk about what happened, and I wasn't sure if it was something she shouldn't hear." Tears pooled in her eyes, and she quickly wiped them away.

Levin nodded, thankful his little sister wasn't there. Crying in front of her would make everything worse, and with his mother already tearing up, he wouldn't get to her house without his grief coming to the surface.

They all loaded into Liz's 4Runner. She wiped her face and turned to Dr. Craig, who took the passenger seat. "Should I drop you off somewhere? I don't know where you're staying."

"I haven't figured that out yet. If you don't mind, I'd like to visit with your family for a while longer."

"Okay." She started the engine. "We'll go back to our house then, after we drop Jason off."

The car was quiet for the first ten minutes of the ride before Liz asked, "So, do you guys want to talk about it? I mean, I assume you defeated Uriah, since you're here."

"Yeah. Levin got Uriah," Rana said as she looked at Levin from the middle seat.

"Really? How?"

Levin looked back at Rana and pondered how much to tell his mother. "With an arrow."

"Oh." She paused. "So what happened to your hand?"

"Um . . . Rana told you about Maggie, right?" His stomach knotted. Having Rana deliver the news hadn't made this conversation easier.

"She told me. Levin, I'm so sorry that happened to you. We'll do whatever we can to help you get through it."

He closed his eyes as tears formed. He was so tired of crying. "Yeah. Okay."

"So what about your hand?" she asked.

He opened his eyes and wiped the tears that escaped with his bandage. "I broke some bones when I beat the crap out of the guy who shot Maggie."

"Oh no." Concern draped his mother's voice. She made eye contact with Levin in the rear-view mirror. "The police are looking for you."

"We know," Dr. Craig said. "I walked in on the scene when it happened. That's why I'm here. I'm hoping that if Peter talks, my testimony will work in Levin's favor."

198

"Should he wait until Peter talks? Would it be better if he turned himself in?"

Dr. Craig twisted around to face the back seat. "It might not be a bad idea. It would show you have nothing to hide."

Levin sat up straighter. "Are you kidding? I have everyone in the Project to hide. How do we explain knowing about Peter being at the church?"

"Maybe he called you to taunt you," Rana said.

"Taunt me? He was mad because he blamed me for Scott's death. We can't talk about that without bringing Mom into it. It just gets worse." He clenched his fist. "Maggie's parents think I was in California when she died. They wouldn't take it well if they found out I was with her at the time." He stared out the window at the passing buildings.

"If he talks, they'll find out anyway," Jason said.

"I know." Levin kept his gaze out the window.

They rode in silence the rest of the way to Jason's house. Liz waited in Jason's driveway long enough to watch Jason's mother open the front door for him, yell in surprise, hug him, and pull him into the house. Jason could count on a celebratory evening.

In fact, all of the others would be celebrating tonight. Levin was alone in dreading his return home.

****

"Oh wow!" Rana's jaw dropped as Liz pulled into the driveway. "The yard looks amazing!"

Apparently, Walt had been busy in their absence. Emerald-green grass that had started to go dormant covered the former dirt patch, and perennials lined the driveway and the path to the front door. A new tree grew in the middle of the yard.

Liz parked the car and shut off the engine. "Yeah, Walt's done some nice things with it. I think he wanted it to be a 'welcome home' present for all of us."

"How did it look before?" Dr. Craig asked.

"Imagine dirt," Rana said.

He chuckled.

They entered the house. Dayla ran at full speed from the kitchen to the front door and wrapped her arms around Rana.

"Hey, girlie." Rana leaned over her sister, stroking her hair. Warmth filled her. She was finally home, and they were all together again. Closing her eyes, she pretended Levin was simply here for dinner–no delusional leaders had wanted to control them, and Maggie was alive–maybe she had to work tonight. For a moment, Rana and her family were a regular family enjoying their time together.

Walt approached behind Dayla and hugged Levin. "Glad to have you back." It seemed the cleaner appearance he adopted before they left two months ago had stuck. His blond hair and clothes were clean, and he had shaved, but it was more than that. His eyes were brighter than Rana had ever seen.

"Thanks, Walt." Levin ran his hand through his hair.

Walt held a hand out to Dr. Craig. "Hi there. I'm Walt. The kids' stepdad."

Dr. Craig shook Walt's hand. "Steven Craig. Nice to meet you."

Dayla released Rana, and the group walked to the kitchen and sat around the table. Liz and Walt busied themselves with fetching drinks and preparing dinner. Dr. Craig excused himself to go outside and make some calls.

"So, how are your brothers doing? Did they all fare okay?" Liz set drinks on the table.

"Yeah. Uriah's the only one who didn't make it out," Levin said.

"And no injuries?"

Rana sipped her tea and set down the glass. "Nothing serious. Daniel got hit in the nose pretty hard, but it wasn't broken. We had to stitch a few cuts. Destiny had a deep one on her arm. And Dante had one on his forehead that I stitched up." Heat rushed to her face in an instant. She sipped her tea again.

"Why are you blushing? Are you warm?" Liz asked.

Levin laughed. "No, that has a different cause."

Rana hit him on the arm.

"Oh, really?" Liz sat in a chair, put her elbow on the table, and leaned her chin into her palm. "Out with it."

Rana pressed her lips together. "Mom! Seriously."

Liz raised her eyebrows.

"Dante and I kinda hit it off when we were in San Diego."

"Kind of hit it off?" Levin looked to his mother. "He asked my permission to date her."

Liz's eyes widened. "He asked for permission? I like him already! Where does he live?"

"Arizona. We exchanged contact info. We'll see how it goes." She couldn't suppress the smile that insisted on occupying her face.

Everyone stared at her, including Walt.

"Will you all please get a life?"

They laughed.

****

"You wanna talk about it?" Walt asked Levin as they sat in neighboring recliners in the family room.

"Talk about what?" Levin grabbed a magazine from the end table, hoping to stall until his mother returned from dropping off Dr. Craig at his hotel. He didn't want to talk about anything. He wished his sisters had stayed downstairs so Walt wouldn't broach the subject.

"About what happened to Maggie. Your mother thought I might be able to help."

Levin looked at him. "I don't think anybody can help."

"You don't think so? You know what happened when I was overseas?"

"A little."

"Well," he focused on his hands, "I watched my buddy get blown to bits four feet from me. Dumb luck it was him and not me." He returned his attention to Levin. "I live with the guilt of that every day. Took your mother threatening to leave me before I talked to anyone about it. Figured I could work through it myself. Didn't get into counseling 'til four years after it happened."

Levin remembered the years he'd cared for his sisters as a father might, when none of them understood why Walt couldn't do something as

202

simple as leave his room. "Well, you do seem different."

"Damn straight. Take it from me: don't live in a personal hell just because you survived. It ruins everything around you–"

"It's not because I survived."

"So what is it?"

Levin faced forward and pressed his lips together. He closed his eyes. "I didn't save her," he started through the shaking in his voice. He twisted in the chair, facing Walt. "I was right there. If I had just kicked faster, or shook the other guys off sooner . . ." Tears stole his words. He continued speaking through clenched teeth, not letting his emotions interrupt what he had to say. "She trusted me. Completely. She trusted me with her life and I didn't save her."

He flopped back into the recliner and wiped his tears with his bandage.

Walt broke the silence that followed. "Do you dream about it?"

"Yeah. Every time I fall asleep. She's screaming. I can't get to her." He kept his eyes on the ceiling, on the magazine–anywhere but on his stepdad.

"Levin, look at me."

Sighing, he turned.

Walt was leaning towards him, over one arm of his chair. "I lost four years to the dreams. The nightmares. When I married your mother, I promised not to just be a husband to her, but a father to you and the girls. I failed miserably on both accounts for years because I let the nightmares control me. Please, don't lose time like I did."

Levin stared at Walt, unsure of how to respond. The front door creaked open from the other side of the house, and Liz's voice broke the silence. "You ready to go, Levin?"

"Yeah." His scratchy voice betrayed the emotional stability he tried to fake.

Rising from the recliner, he looked back to Walt. "Thanks." He jogged up the short flight of stairs to the kitchen and towards the front door before Walt responded.

Epilogue

Dear Maggie,

The counselor said I should keep a journal. I'm not sure what to write. I've been seeing the guy for months and haven't started it yet. He said I can say whatever I want. I'm tired of the nightmares, so I'll give it a shot. Writing to you seems like the way to do it.

I guess I'll start with the funeral. They had pictures of you on tables at the reception. Your mom put out the scrapbook you put together. The one about us. She gave it to me. I put it under my bed but haven't been able to look at it. It feels like I just lost you yesterday.

Dr. Craig stuck around for a couple of weeks before he finally went back to San Diego. I'm not sure what he's doing there. Peter never talked. He's sitting in jail. He pleaded not guilty. I may still be pulled into it before the trial is over.

I'm sorry I didn't save you.

Levin squeezed the pen.

Dr. Craig kept saying things about another group or something that may try to take us out. He

205

wasn't very specific. Rana's planning to visit Dante in Arizona in a few weeks, and part of me wonders if that's a good idea. In any case, I'm sure they can take care of themselves if something happens.

He shook his pen as he considered whether to write his next thought.

I wish I weren't different. I wish PR didn't exist. But I guess that means I wouldn't exist. That would have been better for you.

He stopped writing, crumpled the paper, and threw it into the garbage. "This is stupid."

He went to his room to change into his workout clothes. He left his apartment and walked through the falling snow to the gym after deciding to skip dinner. Martial arts kept his mind off the nightmares. Eating didn't do much for him except make his stomach turn.

Why did he bother to stay engaged in his life at all? It would be so easy to check out the way Walt did and simply exist. In his lowest moments, he found himself doing the same thing: he pulled Dayla's note, harboring dozens of names and phone numbers, from his wallet.

If Dr. Craig was right, and another group threatened his peers–his family–again, it would be Levin's responsibility to get them to safety. They were counting on him. They just didn't know it.

He didn't have the luxury of checking out from his life.

The End

Continued in Project Ancora

Did you enjoy the story? Head to the book's Amazon page and write a review! Readers like you make a big difference to writers like me. Thanks in advance!

Acknowledgements

After three years, seeing this book come to life brings me great joy, and it would not have been possible without the help and encouragement of some key people.

To my writing partner, editor, and friend, Dan Alatorre, I can't thank you enough for the myriad of ways you support me, my work, and my social media presence. I can say with absolute certainty that I would not be where I am today without you.

To my writing partner and friend, Carol Bellhouse, I offer my sincere thanks for the ways you've helped me grow as a writer and for making this book and the trilogy possible now. I also thank you for helping me work out the legal details contained in this volume.

To the fans of the first volume, Project Renovatio, I thank you for your enthusiasm and for sharing the book with your friends. You give me great confidence that this trilogy can do something special.

And finally, to my husband, Joe, and our sons, Nathan and Silas, thank you for allowing me to live this amazing and sometimes bizarre dream, for putting up with writer speak on road trips, and for celebrating every achievement with me. I couldn't do this without your support.

Other Books by Allison Maruska

Project Renovatio

Levin Davis has it made. At 20, he's a college graduate with a dream job, a beautiful girlfriend, and a life that can only get better - until he receives a mysterious letter suggesting his long-dead father is alive and hiding an extraordinary secret.

Distraught, Levin meets the letter's author, who could pass for his twin. The stranger claims to be part of a genetically engineered race designed to survive global catastrophes and rebuild society, and he insists Levin and his sisters are as well.

Despite his disbelief, Levin uncovers not only the bizarre truth of his existence but also Project Renovatio's ominous purpose – to secure genetic superiority, the new race must live according to harsh demands or risk severe penalties inflicted on their loved ones. If Levin hopes to protect his family and live a free life, he must escape Project Renovatio – or rise above himself to fight them.

"What if scientists take genetic engineering to the next level and start altering the human race? Allison Maruska writes a thrilling YA novel that will grab the attention of her readers and hold it until the end."
– Lisa Tortorello, author of My Hero, My Ding

Drake and the Fliers

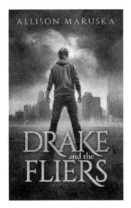

Sixteen-year-old Drake can't understand why the virus spared him. The only survivors he's seen vandalized his makeshift dwelling, and despite his sister's dying wish that he connect with others, he spends his days alone – that is, until he shapeshifts into a dragon.

While exploring his new abilities, Drake nearly flies into Preston, another shifter. Their chances of survival increase if they team up with others like them, but when their search leads to a group in Las Vegas, they find not everyone is welcoming.

As Drake develops new relationships, Preston endures daily confrontation and eventually takes off on his own. Concerned for his friend's safety, Drake launches a search and stumbles into a situation stranger than anything he could imagine. Now he must embrace his animalism if he wants to save his humanity.

"Maruska does a stellar job of creating believable characters that are flawed and relatable but also admirable in their determination."
– Allison Gammons, author and blogger for Eclectic Alli

The Fourth Descendant

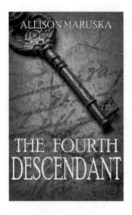

When Michelle receives a call from a Richmond historian, she sees the chance for a much-needed adventure. All she has to do is find a century-old key.

Three others – a guitarist, an engineer, and a retiree – receive similar calls. Each family possesses a key to a four-lock safe found buried in a Virginia courthouse, though their connection is as mysterious as the safe itself. Their ancestors should not have interacted, had no apparent reason to bury the safe, and should not have disappeared thereafter.

Bearing their keys, Michelle and the other descendants converge in the courthouse basement and open the safe, revealing the truth about their ancestors - a truth stranger, more deadly, and potentially more world-changing than any of them could have imagined. Now it's up to them to keep their discovery out of the wrong hands.

"I rarely read a story that I can't wait to get back to, and this was one. It's full of drama and suspense. It's fresh and new, something very much needed, and it's totally unpredictable."
- John Darryl Winston, author of IA: Initiate

About the Author

Allison Maruska started her writing adventure in 2012 as a humor blogger. Her first published book, a historical mystery novel called The Fourth Descendant, was released in February, 2015. Drake and the Fliers followed in November, 2015. Project Renovatio was released in April, 2016, with the other two parts of the trilogy scheduled for release by the end of the year.

Allison recently transitioned to a full-time writing career after working for thirteen years in elementary education. She's also a wife, mom, coffee and wine consumer, and owl enthusiast.

Connect with Allison on the interwebs!

Blog: http://www.allisonmaruska.com

Facebook:
http://www.facebook.com/allisonmaruskaauthor

Twitter: https://twitter.com/allisonmaruska

Amazon Author Page:
http://amazon.com/author/allisonmaruska

Made in the USA
Columbia, SC
22 November 2021